Wednesday the Tenth, A Tale of the South Pacific by Grant Allen

Charles Grant Blairfindie Allen was born on February 24th, 1848 at Alwington, near Kingston, Canada West (now part of Ontario).

Home schooled until 13 when his family moved to England, Grant was to become a highly regarded science writer who branched out to a fiction career and became enormously popular.

His work helped propel several genres of fiction and whilst his career was short it was enormously productive.

Grant's scientific background enabled him to root much of his work in a plausibility that was denied to others. He had little fear in challenging a society that treated women as second class citizens and creating best sellers from such works.

On October 25th 1899 Grant Allen died at his home in Hindhead, Haslemere, Surrey, England. He died just before finishing Hilda Wade. The novel's final episode, which he dictated to his friend, doctor and neighbour Sir Arthur Conan Doyle from his bed appeared under the appropriate title, The Episode of the Dead Man Who Spoke in 1900.

Index of Contents
CHAPTER I - WE SIGHT A BOAT
CHAPTER II - THE BOAT'S CREW
CHAPTER III - THE MYSTERY SOLVED
CHAPTER IV - MARTIN LUTHER'S STORY
CHAPTER V - A BREAK-DOWN
CHAPTER VI - ON THE ISLAND
CHAPTER VII - ERRORS EXCEPTED
CHAPTER VIII - HOT WORK
GRANT ALLEN - A SHORT BIOGRAPHY
GRANT ALLEN - A CONCISE BIBLIOGRAPHY

CHAPTER I

WE SIGHT A BOAT

On the eighteenth day out from Sydney, we were cruising under the lee of Erromanga, of course you know Erromanga, an isolated island between the New Hebrides and the Loyalty group, when suddenly our dusky Polynesian boy, Nassaline, who was at the masthead on the lookout, gave a surprised cry of "Boat ahoy!" and pointed with his skinny black finger to a dark dot away southward on the horizon, in the direction of Fiji.

I strained my eyes and saw, well, a barrel or something. For myself, I should never have made out it was a boat at all, being somewhat slow of vision at great distances; but, bless your heart! these Kanaka lads have eyes like hawks for pouncing down upon a canoe or a sail no bigger than a speck afar off; so when Nassaline called out confidently, "Boat ahoy!" in his broken English, I took out my binocular, and focused it full on the spot towards which the skinny black finger pointed. Probably, thought I to myself, a party of natives, painted red, on the war-trail against their enemies in some neighboring island; or perhaps a "labor vessel," doing a veiled slave-trade in "indentured apprentices" for New Caledonia or the Queensland planters.

To my great surprise, however, I found out, when I got my glasses fixed full upon it, it was neither of these, but an open English row-boat, apparently, making signs of distress, and alone in the midst of the wide Pacific.

Now, mind you, one doesn't expect to find open English row-boats many miles from land, drifting about casually in those far-eastern waters. There's very little European shipping there of any sort, I can tell you; a man may sometimes sail for days together across that trackless sea without so much as speaking a single vessel, and the few he does come across are mostly engaged in what they euphoniously call "the labor-trade"—in plain English, kidnaping blacks or browns, who are induced to sign indentures for so many years' service (generally "three yams," that is to say, for three yam crops), and are then carried off by force or fraud to some other island, to be used as laborers in the cane-fields or cocoa-nut groves. So I rubbed my eyes when I saw an open boat, of European build, tossing about on the open, and sang out to the man at the wheel:

"Hard a starboard, Tom! Put her head about for the dark spot to the sou'-by-southeast there!"

"Starboard it is!" Tom Blake answered cheerily, setting the rudder about; and we headed straight for that mysterious little craft away off on the horizon.

But there! I see I've got ahead of my story, to start with, as the way is always with us salt-water sailors. We seafaring men can never spin a yarn, turned straight off the reel all right from the beginning, like some of those book-making chaps can do. We have always to luff round again, and start anew on a fresh tack half a dozen times over, before we can get well under way for the port we're aiming at. So I shall have to go back myself to Sydney once more, to explain who we were, and how we happened to be cruising about on the loose that morning off Erromanga.

My name, if I may venture to introduce myself formally, is Julian Braithwaite. I am the owner and commander of the steam-yacht Albatross, thirty-nine tons burden, as neat a little craft as any on the Pacific, though it's me that says it as oughtn't to say it; and I've spent the last five years of my life in cruising in and out among those beautiful archipelagos in search of health, which nature denies me in more northern latitudes. The oddest part of it is, though I'm what the doctors call consumptive in England, only fit to lie on a sofa and read good books, the moment I get clear away into the Tropics I'm a strong man again, prepared to fight any fellow of my own age and weight, and as fit for seamanship as the best Jack Tar in my whole equipment. The Albatross numbers eighteen in crew, all told; and as I am not a rich enough or selfish enough a man to keep up a vessel all for my own amusement, my brother Jim and I combine business and pleasure by doing a mixed trade in copra or dried cocoa-nut with the natives from time to time, or by running across between Sydney and San Francisco with a light cargo of goods for the Australian market.

Our habit was therefore to cruise in and out among the islands, with no very definite aim except that of picking up a stray trade whenever we could make one, and keeping as much within sight of land, for the sake of company, as circumstances permitted us. And that is just why, though bound for Fiji, we had gone so far out of our way that particular voyage as to be under the lee of Erromanga.

As for our black Polynesian boy, Nassaline, to tell you the truth, I am proud of that lad, for he's a trophy of war; we got him at the point of the sword off a slaver. She was a fast French sloop, "recruiting" for New Caledonia, as they call it, on one of the New Hebrides, when the Albatross happened to come to anchor, by good luck or good management, in the same harbor. From the moment we arrived I had my eye on that smart French sloop, for I more than half suspected the means she was employing to beat up recruits. Early next morning, as I lay in my bunk, I heard a fearful row going on in boats not far from our moorings; and when I rushed up on deck, half-dressed, to find out what the noise was about, blessed if I didn't see whole gangs of angry natives in canoes, naked of course as the day they were born, or only dressed, like the Ancient Britons, in a neat coat of paint, pursuing the French sloop's jolly-boat, which was being rowed at high pressure by all its crew toward its own vessel. "Great guns!" said I, "what's up?" So, looking closer, I could make out four strapping young black boys lying manacled in the bottom, kicking and screaming as hard as their legs and throats could go, while the Frenchmen rowed away for dear life, and the Kanakas in the canoes paddled wildly after them, taking cock-shots at them with very bad aim from time to time with arrows and fire-arms. Such a splutter and noise you never heard in all your life. Ducks fighting in a pond were a mere circumstance to it.

"Tom Blake!" I sang out, "is the gig afloat there?"

"Aye, aye, sir," says Tom, jumping up. "She's ready at the starn. Shall we off and at 'em?"

"Right you are, Tom!" says I; "all hands to the gig here!"

Well, in less than three minutes I'd got that boat under way, and was rowing ahead between the Frenchmen and their sloop, with our Remingtons ready, and everything in order for a good stand-up fight of it.

When the Frenchmen saw we meant to intercept them, and found themselves cut off between the savages on one side and an English crew well-armed with rifles of precision on the other, they thought it was about time to open negotiations with the opposing party. So the skipper stopped, as airy as a gentleman walking down the Boulevards, and called out to me in French, "What do you want ahoy, there?"

"Ahoy there yourself," says I, in my very best Ollandorff. "We want to know what you're doing with those youngsters?"

"Oh! it's that, is it?" says the Frenchman, as cool as a cucumber, coming nearer a bit, and talking as though we'd merely stopped him with polite inquiries about the time of day or the price of spring chickens; while the savages, seeing from our manner we were friendly to their side, left off firing for a while for fear of hitting us. "Why, these are apprentices of ours—indentured apprentices. We've bought them from their parents by honest trade, paid for 'em with Sniders, ammunition, calico and tobacco; and if you want to see our papers and theirs, Monsieur, here they are, look you, all perfectly en règle," and he held up the bundle for us to inspect in full, with a telescope, I suppose, at a hundred yards' distance.

"Row nearer, boys," I said, "and we'll talk a bit with this polite gentleman. He seems to have views of his own, I fancy, about the proper method of engaging servants."

But when we tried to row up the Frenchman stopped and called out at the top of his voice, in a very different tone, all bustle and bluster, "Look out ahead there! If you come a yard closer we open fire. We want no interference from any of you Methodistical missionary fellows."

"We ain't missionaries," I answered quietly, cocking my revolver in the friendliest possible fashion right in front of him; "we're traders and yachtsmen. Show 'em your Remingtons, boys, and let 'em see we mean business! That's right. Ready! present!—and fire when I tell you! Now then, Monsieur, you bought these boys, you say. So far, good. Next then, if you please, who did you buy them from?"

The Frenchman turned pale when he saw we were well-armed and meant inquiry; but he tried to carry off still with a little face and bluster. "Why, their parents, of course," he answered, with a signal to his friends in the ship to cover us with their fire-arms.

"From their parents? O, yes! Well, how did you know the sellers were their parents?" I asked, still pointing my revolver towards him. "And why are the boys so unwilling to go? And what are the natives making such a noise over this little transaction in indentured labor for? If it's all as you say, what's this fuss and row about? Keep your rifles steady, lads."

"They want to back out of their bargain, I suppose, now they've drunk our rum and smoked our tobacco," the Frenchman said.

"No true, no true," one of the natives shouted out from beyond in his broken English. "Man a oui-oui!"—that's what they call the French, you know, all through the South Pacific—"man a oui-oui, bad, no believe man, a oui-oui, him make us drunk, so try to cheat us."

"Now, you look here, Monsieur," I said severely, turning to the skipper, "I know what you've been doing. I've seen this little game tried on before. You landed here last night with your peaceable equipment for recruiting labor, we know what that means, a Winchester sixteen-shooter and half a dozen pairs of English handcuffs. You brought on shore your 'trade'—a common clay pipe or two, some cheap red cloth, and a lot of bad French Government tobacco; and you treated the natives all round to free drinks of your square gin. When they'd reached that state of convenient conviviality that they didn't know who they were or what they were doing, you took advantage of their guileless condition. You picked out the likeliest young men and lads, selected any particularly drunken native lying about loose to represent their fathers, made 'em put their marks to a formal paper of indentures, and handed over twenty dollars, a bottle of rum, and a quid of tobacco, as a consolation for the wounded feelings of their distressed relations. You've been carrying them off all night at your devil's game; and now in the morning the natives are beginning to wake up sober, miss their friends, and put a summary stop to your little proceedings. Well, sir, I give you one minute to make up your mind; if you don't hand us over these four lads to set on shore again, we'll open fire upon you; and as we're stronger than you, with the natives at our back, we'll make a prize of you, and tow you into Fiji on a charge of slave-trading."

Before the words were well out of my mouth the French skipper had given the word "Fire!" and the bullets came whizzing past, and riddling the gunwale of the gig beside us. One of them grazed my arm below the shoulder and drew blood. Now there's nothing to put a man's temper up like getting shot in the arm. I lost mine, I confess, and I shouted aloud, "Fire, boys, and row on at them!" Our fellows fired, and the very same moment the natives closed in and went at them with their canoes, all alive with Sniders, lances and hatchets. It was a lively time, I can tell you, for the next five minutes, with those lithe, long black fellows swarming over them like ants; and poor Tom Blake got a bullet from a French rifle in his thigh, that lodges there still in very comfortable quarters. But one of the Frenchmen fell back in the jolly-boat shot through the breast, and the skipper, who turned out to be a fellow with one sound leg and a substitute, was severely wounded. So we'd soon closed in upon them, the natives and ourselves, and overpowered their crew, which was only ten, all told, besides the fellows on the big vessel in the harbor.

Well, we took out the four boys, when the mill was over, and transferred them to our gig; and then we escorted the Frenchmen, ironed in their own handcuffs, to the deck of their sloop, with the natives on either side in their canoes rowing along abreast of us like a guard of honor. The crew of the sloop didn't attempt to interfere with us as we brought their comrades handcuffed aboard; if they had, why, then, with the help of the savages, we should have been more than a match for them. So we prowled around the ship on a voyage of discovery, and found ample evidence in her get-up of her character as an honest and single-hearted recruiter of labor. A rack in the cabin held eight Snider rifles, loaded for use, above which hung eight revolvers, employed doubtless in self-defense against the lawless character of the Kanakas, as the skipper (with his hands in irons and his eyes in tears) most solemnly assured us. The sloop was prepared throughout, with loopholes and battening-hatches, to stand a siege, and could have made short work of the natives alone had they tried to attack her, for she carried a small howitzer, not so big as our own; but she never suspected interference from a European vessel. We went down into her hold, and there we found about forty natives, men, women and children, free agents all, the skipper had declared, packed as tight as herrings in a barrel, and with stench intolerable to the European nostril. Such a sight you never saw in your life. There they lay athwart ship, side by side, the unhappy black cattle, some handcuffed and manacled, others dead-drunk and too careless to complain, while the women and children were crying and screaming, and the men were shouting as loud as they could shout in their own lingo.

Fortunately, we had a sailor aboard the Albatross who had been a beach-comber (or degraded white man who lives like a native) for three years on the island of Ambrymon, and had a Kanaka girl for a sweetheart; so he could talk their palaver almost as easy as you can English, and he acted as interpreter for us with the poor people in the hold. We knocked their handcuffs off, and explained the situation to them. About a dozen of the wretchedest and most squalid-looking of the lot were prepared, even when we offered them freedom, to stand by their last night's bargain, and go on to New Caledonia; but the remainder were only too delighted to learn that they might go ashore again; and they gave us three ringing British cheers as soon as they understood we had really liberated them.

As for the four boys we'd got in the gig, three of them elected at once to go home to their own people on the island; but the fourth was our present black servant, Nassaline. He, poor boy, was an orphan; and his nearest relations, having held a consultation the day before whether they should bake him and eat him, or sell him to the Frenchman, had decided that after all he would be worth more if paid for in tobacco and rum than if roasted in plantain-leaves. So, as soon as he found we were going to put him on shore again, the poor creature was afraid after all he was being returned for the oven; and flinging himself on his face in the gig, groveling and cringing, he took hold of our knees and besought us most piteously (as our sailor translated his words for us) to take him with us. Of course, when we entered into the spirit of the situation, we felt it was impossible to send the poor fellow back to be made "long pig" of; so, to his immense delight, we took him along, and a more faithful servant no man ever had than poor Nassaline proved from that day forth to me.

I've gone out of my way so far, as I said before, to tell you this little episode of life in the South Pacific, partly in order to let you know who Nassaline was and how we came by him; but partly also to give you a side glimpse of the sort of gentry, both European and native, one may chance to knock up against in those remote regions. It'll help you to understand the rest of my yarn. And now, if you please, I'll tack back again once more into my proper course, to the spot where I broke off in sight of Erromanga.

CHAPTER II

Presently, as we headed towards the black object on the horizon, Nassaline stretched out that skinny finger of his once more (no amount of feeding ever seemed to make Nassaline one ounce fatter), and cried out in his shrill little piping voice, "Two man on the boat! him makey signs for call us!"

I'd give anything to have eyes as sharp as those Polynesians. I looked across the sea, and the loppy waves in the foreground, and could just make out with the naked eye that the row-boat had something that looked like a red handkerchief tied to her bare mast, and a white signal flapping in the wind below it; but not a living soul could I distinguish in her without my binocular. So I put up my glasses and looked again. Sure enough, there they were, two miserable objects, clinging as it seemed half-dead to the mast, and making most piteous signs with their hands to attract our attention. As soon as they saw that we had really sighted them, and were altering our course to pick them up, their joy and delight knew no bounds, as we judged. They flung up their arms ecstatically into the air, and then sank back, exhausted, as I guessed, on to the thwarts where they had long ceased sitting or rowing.

They were wearied out, I imagined, with long buffeting against that angry and immeasurable sea, and must soon have succumbed to fatigue if we hadn't caught sight of them.

We put on all steam, as in duty bound, and made towards them hastily. By and by, my brother Jim, who had been off watch, came up from below and joined me on deck to see what was going forward. At the same moment Nassaline cried out once more, "Him no two man! Him two boy! Two English boy! Him hungry like a dying!" And as he spoke, he held his own skinny bare arm up to his mouth dramatically, and took a good bite at it, as if to indicate in dumb show that the crew of the boat were now almost ready to eat one another.

Jim looked through the glasses, and handed them over to me in turn. "By George, Julian," he said, "Nassaline's right. It's a couple of boys, and to judge by the look of them, they're not far off starving!"

I seized the glasses and fixed them upon the boat. We were getting nearer now, and could make out the features of its occupants quite distinctly. A more pitiable sight never met my eyes. Her whole crew consisted of two white-faced lads, apparently about twelve or thirteen years old, dressed in loose blue cotton shirts and European trousers, but horribly pinched with hunger and thirst, and evidently so weak as to be almost incapable of clinging to the bare mast whence they were trying to signal us.

Now, you land-loving folk can hardly realize, I dare say, what such an incident means at sea; but to Jim and me, who had sailed the lonely Pacific together for five years at a stretch, that pathetic sight was full both of horror and unspeakable mystery. For anybody, even grown men long used to the ocean, to be navigating that awful expanse of water alone in an empty boat is little short of ghastly. Just think what it means! A stormy sheet that stretches from the north pole to the south without one streak of continuous land to break it; a stormy sheet on which the winds and waves may buffet you about in almost any direction for five thousand miles, with only the stray chance of some remote oceanic isle to drift upon, or some coral reef to swallow you up with its gigantic breakers. But a couple of boys!—mere children almost!—alone, and starving, on that immense desert of almost untraveled water! On the Atlantic itself your chance of being picked up from open boats by a passing vessel is slight enough, heaven knows! but on the Pacific, where ships are few and routes are far apart, your only alternative to starvation or foundering is to find yourself cast on the tender mercies of the cannibal Kanaka. No wonder I looked at Jim, and Jim looked at me, and each of us saw unaccustomed tears standing half ashamed in the eyes of the other.

"Stop her!" I cried. "Lower the gig, Tom Blake! Jim, we must go ourselves and fetch these poor fellows."

At the sound of my bell the engineer pulled up the Albatross short and sharp, with admirable precision, and we lowered our boat to go out and meet them. As we drew nearer and nearer with each stroke of our oars, I could see still more plainly to what a terrible pitch of destitution and distress these poor lads had been subjected during their awful journey. Their cheeks were sunken, and their eyes seemed to stand back far in the hollow sockets. Their pallid white hands hardly clung to the mast by convulsive efforts with hooked fingers. They had used up their last reserve of strength in their wild efforts to attract our attention.

I thanked heaven it was Nassaline who kept watch at the mast-head when they first hove in sight. No European eye could ever have discovered the meaning of that faint black speck upon the horizon. If it hadn't been for the sharp vision of our keen Polynesian friend, these two helpless children might have drifted on in their frail craft for ever, till they wasted away with hunger and thirst under the broiling eye of the hot Pacific noontide.

We pulled alongside, and lifted them into the gig. As we reached them, both boys fell back faint with fatigue and with the sudden joy of their unexpected deliverance. "Quick, quick, Jim! your flask!" I cried, for we had brought out a little weak brandy and water on purpose. "Pour it slowly down their throats, not too fast at first, just a drop at a time, for fear of choking them."

Jim held the youngest boy's head on his lap, and opened those parched lips of his that looked as dry as a piece of battered old shoe-leather. The tongue lolled out between the open teeth like a thirsty dog's at midsummer, and was hard and rough as a rasp with long weary watching. We judged the lad at sight to be twelve years old or thereabouts. Jim put the flask to his lips, and let a few drops trickle slowly down his burnt throat. At touch of the soft liquid the boy's lips closed over the mouth of the flask with a wild movement of delight, and he sucked in eagerly, as you may see a child in arms suck at the mouthpiece of its empty feeding-bottle. "That's well," I said. "He's all right, at any rate. As long as he has strength enough to pull at the flask like that, we shall bring him round in the end somehow."

We took away the flask as soon as we thought he'd had as much as was good for him at the time, and let his head fall back once more upon Jim's kindly shoulder. Now that the first wild flush of delight at their rescue was fairly over, a reaction had set in; their nerves and muscles gave way simultaneously, and the poor lad fell back, half-fainting, half-sleeping, just where Jim with his fatherly solicitude chose to lay him.

Tom Blake and I turned to the elder lad. His was a harder and more desperate case. Perhaps he had tried more eagerly to save his helpless brother; perhaps the sense of responsibility for another's life had weighed heavier upon him at his age, for he looked fourteen; but at any rate he was well-nigh dead with exposure and exhaustion. The first few drops we poured down his throat he was clearly quite unable to swallow. They gurgled back insensibly. Tom Blake took out his handkerchief, and tearing off a strip, soaked it in brandy and water in the cup end of the flask; then he gently moistened the inside of the poor lad's mouth and throat with it, till at last a faint swallowing motion was set up in the gullet. At that, we poured down some five drops cautiously. To our delight and relief they were slowly gulped down, and the poor white mouth stood agape like a young bird's in mute appeal for more water, more water.

We gave him as much as we dared in his existing state, and then turned to the boat for some clue to the mystery.

She was an English-built row-boat, smart and taut, fit for facing rough seas, and carrying a short, stout mast amidships. On her stern we found her name in somewhat rudely-painted letters, Messenger of Peace: Makilolo in Tanaki. Clearly she had been designed for mission service among the islands, and the last words which followed her title must be meant to designate her port, or the mission station. But what that place was I hadn't a notion.

"Where's Tanaki, Tom Blake?" I asked, turning round, for Tom had been navigating the South Seas any time this twenty years, and knew almost every nook and corner of the wide Pacific, from Yokohama to Valparaiso.

Tom shifted his quid from one cheek to the other and answered, after a pause, "Dunno, sir, I'm sure. Never heerd tell of Tanaki in all my born days; an' yet I sorter fancied, too, I knowed the islands."

"There are no signs of blood or fighting in the boat," I said, examining it close. "They can't have escaped from a massacre, anyhow." For I remembered at once to what perils the missionaries are often exposed in these remote islands, how good Bishop Patteson had been murdered at Santa Cruz, and how the natives had broken the heads of Mason and Wood at Erromanga not so many months back, in cold blood, out of pure lust of slaughter.

"But they must have run away in an awful hurry," Tom Blake added, overhauling the locker of the boat, "for, see, she ain't found; there ain't no signs of food or anything to hold it nowheres, sir; and this ere little can must 'a' been the o'ny thing they had with 'em for water."

He was quite right. The boat had clearly put to sea unprovisioned. It deepened our horror at the poor lads' plight to think of this further aggravation of their incredible sufferings. For days they must have tossed in hunger and thirst on the great deep. But we could only wait to have the mystery cleared up when the lads were well enough to explain to us what had happened. Meanwhile we could but look and wonder in silence; and indeed we had quite enough to do for the present in endeavoring to restore them to a state of consciousness.

"Any marks on their clothes?" my brother Jim suggested, with practical good sense, looking up from his charge as we rowed back toward the Albatross, with the Messenger of Peace in tow behind us. "That might help us to guess who they are, and where they hail from."

I looked close at the belt of the lads' blue shirts. On the elder's I read in a woman's handwriting, "Martin Luther Macglashin, 6, '87." The younger boy's bore in the same hand the corresponding inscription, "John Knox Macglashin, 6, '86." It somehow deepened the tragedy of the situation to come upon those simple domestic reminiscences at such a moment.

"Sons of a Scotch missionary, apparently," I said, as I read them out. "If only we could find where their father was at work, we might manage to get some clue to this mystery."

"We can look him up," Jim answered, "when we get to Fiji."

We rowed back in silence the rest of the way to the Albatross, lifted the poor boys tenderly on board, and laid them down to rest on our own bunks in the cabin. Serang-Palo, our Malay cook, made haste at the galleys to dress them a little arrowroot with condensed milk; and before half an hour the younger boy was sitting up in Jim's arms with his eyes and mouth wide open, craving eagerly for the nice warm mess we were obliged to dole out to his enfeebled stomach in sparing spoonfuls, and with a trifle of color already returning to his pale cheeks. He was too ill to speak yet, his brother indeed lay even now insensible on the bunk in the corner, but as soon as he had finished the small pittance of arrowroot which alone we thought it prudent to let him swallow at present, he mustered up just strength enough to gasp out a few words of solemn importance in a very hollow voice. We bent over him to listen. They were broken words we caught, half rambling as in delirium, but we heard them distinctly—

"Steer for Makilolo ... Island of Tanaki ... Wednesday the tenth ... Natives will murder them ... My mother, my father, Calvin, and Miriam."

Then it was evident he could not say another word. He sank back on the pillow breathless and exhausted. The color faded from his cheek once more as he fell into his place. I poured another spoonful of brandy down his parched throat. In three minutes more he was sleeping peacefully, with long even breath, like one who hadn't slept for nights before on the tossing ocean.

I looked at Jim and bit my lips hard. "This is indeed a fix," I cried, utterly nonplussed. "Where on earth, I should like to know, is this island of Tanaki!"

"Don't know," said Jim. "But wherever it is, we've got to get there."

CHAPTER III

THE MYSTERY SOLVED

We paused for a while, and looked at one another's faces blankly.

"Suppose," Jim suggested at last, "we get out the charts and see if such a place as Tanaki is marked upon them anywhere."

"Right you are," says I. "Overhaul your maps, and when found, make a note of."

Well, we did overhaul them for an hour at a stretch, and searched them thoroughly, inch by inch, Jim taking one sheet of the Admiralty chart for the South Pacific, and I the other; but never a name could we find remotely resembling the sound or look of Tanaki. Tom Blake, too, was positive, as he put it himself, that "there weren't no such name, not in the whole thunderin' Pacific, nowheres." So after long and patient search we gave up the quest, and determined to wait for further particulars till the boys had recovered enough to tell us their strange story.

Meanwhile, it was clear we must steer somewhere. We couldn't go beating wildly up and down the Pacific, on the hunt for a possibly non-existent Tanaki, allowing the Albatross to drift at her own sweet will wherever she liked, pending the boys' restoration to speech and health. So the question arose what direction we should steer in. Jim solved that problem as easy as if it had come out of the first book of Euclid (he was always a mathematician, Jim was, while for my part, when I was a little chap at school, the asses' bridge at an early stage effectually blocked my further progress. I could never get over it, even with the persuasive aid of what Dr. Slasher used politely to call his vis a tergo.)

"They're too weak to row far, these lads," Jim said in his didactic way, ought to have been a schoolmaster or a public demonstrator, Jim: such a head for proving things! "Therefore they must mostly have been drifting before the wind ever since they started. Now, wind for the last fortnight's been steadily nor'east"—the anti-trade was blowing. "Therefore, they must have come from the nor'east, I take it; and if we steer clean in the face of the wind, we're bound sooner or later to arrive at Tanaki."

"Jim," said I, admiring him, like, "you're really a wonderful chap. You do put your finger down so pat on things! Steer to the nor'-east it is, of course. But I wonder how far off Tanaki lies, and what chance we've got of reaching there by Wednesday the tenth?" For though we didn't even know yet who the people were who were threatened with massacre at this supposed Tanaki, we couldn't let them have their throats cut in cold blood without at least an attempt to arrive there in time to prevent it.

Of course, we knew with our one brass gun we should be more than a match for any Melanesian islanders we were likely to meet with, if once we could get there; but the trouble was, should we reach in time to forestall the massacre?

By Wednesday the tenth we must reach Tanaki, wherever that might be.

Jim took out a piece of paper and totted up a few figures carelessly on the back. "We've plenty of coal," he said, "and I reckon we can make nine knots an hour, if it comes to a push, even against this head wind. To-day's the sixth; that gives us four clear days still to the good. At nine knots, we can do a run of two hundred and thirty-six knots a day. Four two-hundred-and-thirty-sixes is nine hundred and forty-four, isn't it? Let me see; four sixes is twenty-four; put down four and carry two: four three's is twelve, and two's fourteen: four two's, yes, that's all right: nine hundred and forty-four, you see, ex-actly. Well, then, look here, Julian: unless Tanaki's further off than nine hundred and forty-four nautical miles, which isn't likely, we ought to get there by twelve o'clock on Wednesday at latest. Nine hundred and forty-four miles is an awful long stretch for two boys to come in an open boat. I don't expect these boys can have done as much as that or anything like it."

"Wind and current were with them," I objected, "and she was drifting like one o'clock when we first sighted her. I shouldn't be surprised if she was making five or six knots an hour before half a gale all through that hard blow. And the poor boys look as if they might have been out a week or more. Still, it isn't likely they would have come nine hundred knots, as you say, or anything like it. If we put on all steam, we ought to arrive in time to save their father and mother. Anyhow we'll try it." And I shouted down the speaking tube, "Hi, you there, engineer!—pile on the coal hard and make her travel. We want all the speed we can get out of the Albatross for the next three days."

"All square, sir," says Jenkins; and he piled on, accordingly.

So we steamed ahead as hard as we could go, in the direction where we expected to find Tanaki.

Half an hour later, Nassaline, who had been down below with the Malay cook and one of the men, looking after the patients, came up on deck once more, with a broad grin on his jet-black face from ear to ear, and exclaimed in his very best Kanaka-English, "Boy come round again. Eat plenty arrowroot. Eat allee samee like as if starvee. Call very hard for see Massa Captain."

"What do you think's the matter with them, Nassaline?" I asked, as I walked along by his side towards the companion-ladder.

Nassaline's ideas were exclusively confined to a certain fixed and narrow Polynesian circle. "Tink him fader go sell him for laborer to a man oui-oui, or make oven hot for him," he answered, grinning; "so him run away, and come put himself aboard Massa Captain ship; so eat plenty, no beat, no starvee."

It was his own personal history put in brief, and he fitted it at once as the only possible explanation to these other poor fugitives.

"Nonsense!" I said, with a compassionate smile at his innocence. "White people don't sell or eat their children, stupid! It's my belief, Nassaline, we'll never make a civilized Christian creature of you, in a tall hat, and with a glass in your eye. You ain't cut out for it, somehow. How many times have I explained to you, boy, that Christians never cook and eat their enemies?... They only love them, and blow them up with Gatlings or Armstrongs, a purely fraternal method of expressing slight differences of international opinion.... Now, come along down and let's see these lads. It's some of your heathen relations, I expect, the poor fellows are flying from."

But I omitted to have remarked to him (as I might have done) that I hadn't seen such a painful sight before, since I saw the inhabitants of a French village in Lorraine, old men, young girls, and mothers with babies pressed against their breasts, flying, pell-mell, before the sudden onslaught of a hundred and fifty Christian Prussian Uhlans. These little peculiarities of our advanced civilization are best not mentioned to the heathen Polynesian.

In the cabin we found both boys now fairly on the high-road to recovery, though still, of course, much too weak to talk; but bursting over, for all that, with eagerness to tell us their whole eventful history. For my own part, I, too, was all eagerness to hear it; but anxiety for their safety made me restrain my impatience. The elder boy, now leaning on his elbow and staring wildly before him with horror, a mere skeleton to look at, with his sunken cheeks and great hollow eyes, began to break forth upon me with his long tale in full; but I soon put a stop to that, you may be pretty sure, with most uncompromising promptitude. "My dear Mr. Martin Luther Macglashin," I said severely, giving him the full benefit of all his own various high-sounding names for greater impressiveness, "if you don't lean back this moment upon your pillow, quiet your rolling eye down to everyday proportions, and answer only in the shortest possible words nothing but the plain questions I put to you, hang me, sir, if I don't turn you and John Knox adrift again upon the wild waves, and continue on my course for Levuka in Fiji."

"Why, how did you come to know our names?" he exclaimed, astonished. "You must be as sharp as a lynx, Captain."

"That's not an answer to my question I asked you," I replied with as much sternness as I could put into my voice, looking at the poor fellow's starved white face. "But as a special favor to a deserving fellow-creature, I don't mind telling you. I'm as sharp as a lynx, as you say, and a trifle sharper: for no lynx would have looked for your names on the flap of your shirts—There, that'll do now; don't try to talk; just answer me quietly. Where do you come from, and where do you want us to go to?"

Martin lifted up his face and answered with becoming brevity, "Tanaki."

"That's better!" I said. "That's the sort of way a fellow ought to answer, when he's more than half-starved with a week at sea. But the next thing is, where's Tanaki?"

"It's one of the group that used to be called the Duke of Cumberland's Islands," the boy answered faintly, yet overflowing with eagerness. "They lie just beyond the Ellice Archipelago, nearly on the line of a hundred and eighty, as you go towards the Union Group along the parallel of"....

"Now, my dear boy," I said, "if you run on like that, as I said before, I shall have to turn you adrift again in your open boat at the mercy of the ocean. Do be quiet, won't you, and let me look up your island?"

"We can't be quiet," Master John Knox put in eagerly, "when we know they're going to murder our father and mother and Calvin and Miriam, on Wednesday morning."

"Just you hold your tongue, sir," I said, pushing him down again on his bunk, "and wait till you're spoken to. Now, not another word, either of you, till I've consulted my chart. Jim, hand down the Admiralty sheets again, there's a good fellow, will you?"

Jim handed them down, and we commenced our scrutiny at once. We soon found the Duke of Cumberland's Islands, and as good luck would have it, found we were steering as straight as an arrow for them. The direction of the wind had not misled us. But no such place as Tanaki could we still find anywhere.

"It used to be called 'The Long Reef,'" Martin said, looking up; "but now we call it by the native name, Tanaki."

"Oh! The Long Reef," I said; "why didn't you say so at first? I know that well enough by sight on the chart; but I never heard it called Tanaki before. That accounts, of course, for the milk in the cocoa-nut. Jim, hand along the calipers here, and let's measure out the course. Two—four—six—eight," I went on, looping along line of sailing with the calipers. "A trifle short of eight hundred miles. Say seven hundred and eighty. And we have till Wednesday morning. Well, we ought to do it."

"You'll be in time to save them, then!" the elder boy cried, jumping up once more like a Jack-in-the-box. "You'll be in time to save them!"

"Will you be quiet, if you please?" I said, poking him down again flat, and holding my hand on his mouth. "O, yes! I expect we'll be in time to save them. If only you'll let us alone, and not make such a noise. We can do nine knots an hour easy, under all steam; and that ought to bring us up to Tanaki, as you call it, by Wednesday morning in the very small hours. Let's see, we've got four clear days to do it in."

"Five," the boy answered. "Five. To-day's Friday."

"No, no," I replied curtly. "Will you please shut up? Especially when you only darken counsel with many words. You're out of your reckoning. To-day's Saturday, I tell you."

And in point of fact, indeed, it really was Saturday.

"No, it's Friday," Martin went on with extraordinary persistence.

"Saturday," I repeated. "Knife; scissors: knife; scissors."

"But we got away from Tanaki eight days ago," the boy declared strongly with a very earnest face; "and it was Thursday when we left. I kept count of the days and nights all that awful time we were tossing about on the ocean alone, and I'm sure I'm right. To-day's Friday."

"Jim," I said, turning to my brother, "what day of the week do you make it?"

"Why, Saturday, of course," Jim answered with confidence.

I went to the bottom of the companion-ladder and called out aloud where the boy could hear me, "Tom Blake, what day of the week and month is it?"

"Saturday the sixth, sir," Tom called out.

"There, my boy," I said, turning to him, "you see you're mistaken. You've lost count of the time in this awful journey of yours. I expect you were half unconscious the last day and night. But, good heavens, Jim, just to think of what they've done! They've been out nine days and nights in an open boat, almost without food or drink, and they've come all that incredible distance before the high wind. Except with a ripping good breeze behind them they could never have done it."

"For my part," said Jim, looking up from his chart, "I can hardly understand how they ever did it at all. I declare, I call it nothing short of a miracle!"

And so indeed it was: for it seemed as though the wind had drifted them straight ahead from the moment they started in the exact direction where the Albatross was to meet them.

I'm an old seafaring hand by this time, and I may be superstitious, but I see the finger of fate in such a coincidence as that one.

CHAPTER IV

MARTIN LUTHER'S STORY

For the next two days we went steaming ahead as hard as we could go in a bee-line to the northeastward, in the direction of the Duke of Cumberland's Islands; and it was two days clear before those unfortunate boys, Jack and Martin, for that was what they called one another for short, in spite of their severely theological second names, were in a condition to tell us exactly what had happened, without danger to their shattered nerves and impaired digestions.

When they did manage to speak, both at once, for choice, in their eagerness to get their story out, here's about what their history came to, as we pieced it together, bit by bit, from the things they told us at different times. If I were one of those writing chaps, now, that know how to tell a whole ten years' history, end on end, exactly as it happened, without missing a detail, I'd get it all out for you just as Martin told us; or better still, I'd give it to you in a single connected piece, between inverted commas, as his own words, beginning, "I was born," said he, "in the city of Edinburgh," and so forth, after the regular high-and-dry literary fashion. But how on earth those clever book-making fellows can ever remember a whole long speech, word for word, from beginning to end, I never could make out and never shall, neither. What memories they must have to do it, to be sure! It's my own belief they make it up more than half out of their own heads as they go along, and are perfectly happy if it only just sounds plausible. But anyhow, Martin Luther Macglashin didn't tell us all his story at a single time, or in a connected way; he gave us a bit now and a bit again, with additions from Jack, according as he was able. So being, as I say, no more than a free-and-easy master mariner myself, without skill in literature, I'm not going to try to repeat it all, word for word, to you precisely as it came, but shall just take the liberty of spinning my yarn my own way and letting you have in short the gist and substance of what we gradually got out of our two fugitives.

Well, it seems that Jack and Martin's father was, just as I suspected, a Scotch missionary on the Island of Tanaki. He lived there with another family of missionaries of the same sect, in peace and quiet, as well as with an English merchant of the name of Williams, who traded with the natives for calico, knives, glass beads and tobacco. For a long time things had gone on pretty comfortably in the little settlement; though to be sure the natives did sometimes steal Mr. Macglashin's fowls or threaten to tie Mr. Williams to a cocoa-nut palm and take cock-shots at him with a Snider, out of pure lightness of heart, unless he gave them rum, square gin or brandy. Still, in spite of these playful little eccentricities of the good-humored Kanakas, who will have their joke, murder or no murder, all went as merrily as a wedding bell (as they say in novels) till suddenly one morning a French labor-vessel, I suspect the very one we had intercepted in the act of trying to carry off Nassaline, put into the harbor in search of "apprentices."

She was a very bad lot, from what the boys told us; a genuine slaver of the worst type; and she stirred up a deal of mischief at Makilolo.

On the shore the Chief of Tanaki was drawn up to receive them with all his warriors, tastefully but inexpensively rigged out in a string of blue beads round the neck, an anklet of shells and a head-dress of a single large yellow feather.

"Who are you?" shouts the chief at the top of his voice. "You man a oui-oui?"

"Yes," the Frenchman shouts back in his pigeon-English. "Me de commander of dis French ship. Want to buy boys. Must sell them to us. Tanaki French island. Discovered by Bougainville."

"No, no," says the Chief in pigeon-English again. "Tanaki no belong a man a oui-oui. Tanaki belong a Queenie England. Capitaney Cook find him long time back. My father little fellow then; him see Capitaney, him tell me often. Capitaney Cook no man a oui-oui; him fellow English."

The other natives joined in at once with their loud cry, "Chief speak true. Tanaki belong a Queenie England. Tanaki no belong a man a oui-oui. If man a oui-oui want to take Tanaki, man a Tanaki come out and fight him." And they threw themselves at once into a threatening attitude.

"Have you got any Englishmen here?" the French skipper called out, to make sure of his ground.

"Yes," says the missionary, our boys' father, standing out from the crowd. "Three English families here. Settled on the island. And we deny that this group belongs to the French Republic."

At that the Frenchman pulled back a bit. When he saw there was likely to be opposition, and that his proceedings were watched by three English families, he drew in his horns a little. He knew if he interfered too openly with the missionaries' proceedings, an English gunboat might come along, sooner or later, and overhaul him for fomenting discord on an island known to be under the British protectorate. So he only answered in French, "Well, we're peaceable traders, Monsieur. We don't want to interfere with the British Government. Consider us friends. All we desire is to hire laborers." And he landed his boat's crew before the very face of Macglashin and the Tanaki warriors.

At first, as often happens in these islands, the natives were very little disposed to trade with the strangers in boys or women, for they were afraid of the Frenchmen; and Macglashin and the other missionary did all they knew to prevent the new comers from carrying off any of the islanders into practical slavery. But after awhile the Frenchmen produced their regulation bottles of square gin (that's what they call Hollands in the South Pacific), and began to treat the Chief and the other savages to drinks all round, as much as you liked, with nothing to pay for it. In a very short time the Chief had got so much liquor aboard that his legs wouldn't answer the rudder any longer, and he began to reel about like a perfect madman. Most of the other full-grown men natives followed suit before long, and lay down on the beach half dead with drunkenness. Perhaps the liquor was drugged; perhaps it wasn't; but anyhow, in spite of all the missionaries could do, the shore before nightfall was in a condition of the wildest and most bestial orgies. The men, in what the newspapers call "a high state of vinous exhilaration," were ready to sell their boys and girls, or anything else on earth for a little more gin; and as the missionaries were naturally helpless to prevent it, the Frenchman was soon driving a roaring trade in flesh and blood against the drunken savages.

The business-like way they went to work, Jack and Martin told us, was horribly disgusting. The women, indeed, they tried to wheedle and cajole—"You like go along a New Caledonia along a me? Only three yam times; then ship bring you back again. Very good feed; plenty nyam-nyam. Pay very good. Pay money. Lots of shop. You buy what you like: you buy red dress, red handkerchief, beads like-a-chiefie. No fight; no beat; no swear at you. You good girl; I good fellow master." But if they couldn't induce them, by fair words and promises and little presents of cheap French finery, to put their mark to their sham indentures, then they just knocked them down with a blow on the head, dragged them by their hair to the boats hard by, and got their fathers or husbands to put their marks, and receive a few dollars and some red cloth in payment.

As for the boys, they handled them like so many animals in a market. "Turn round, cochon! Show me your faces! Mille tonnerres, let me see how you can run, you dirty young blackguard!" They examined them as a veterinary would examine a horse. "Why, there was our little fellow, Nangaree," Jack said to us with deep concern—"Nangaree, that used to clean up things for mother at the mission-house: his father sold him for twenty dollars. The captain looked at his legs, and at the glands in his throat, to see if he'd had the chicken-pox and the measles. Then he said to his mate, 'This lot's cheap enough. He's a first-rate lad, and can speak English. He'll do for the hold. Bundle him along!' And the mate caught him up by the scruff of his neck and hauled him to the boats, kicking and screaming; and that was the last we saw of poor Nangaree!"

For three days and nights, it seems, this horrible inhuman market or slave-fair went on upon the beach, the Frenchmen taking care to keep the natives well primed with spirits all the time, till they'd got their hold full, and were prepared to sail away again with their living cargo. Then at last they upped anchor, and out of the harbor. But before they went, the skipper, it appears, who was angry at the missionaries for having interfered with him, and was afraid they might report his proceedings to the British Government when next the mission ship came that way on her provisioning rounds, took aside the Chief in a confidential chat, and tried to inflame his mind, all mad drunk that he was, against the English residents. Apparently he had made so good a three days' work of it with his horrible trade, and found it so convenient to draw his supplies from this remote and almost unvisited island, that he thought it would be nice if before his next visit he could get rid altogether of these meddlesome strangers. He didn't want European witnesses to crop up against him in future; so he told the Chief, with a great show of confidence, that Macglashin and his friends were not English at all, but Scotch; and he pointed out that it was uncomfortable for the natives to be interfered with in their trading operations by a set of white-livered curs who objected to the selling of boys and girls into temporary slavery. Surely a Chief had a right to do as he would with his own subjects! What else he said, Heaven knows, but this is what happened as soon as the French, with their horrid cargo, had got well clear of the unhappy island.

That very afternoon, the Chief, beginning to get sober again, but quarrelsome from headache and the other after-effects of a long debauch, came round to the mission-house in a towering rage, and asked the unsuspecting missionary, "Say, white man, are you a Scotchman?"

"Yes," says Macglashin, not knowing what was coming. "I'm a Scotchman, Chief, certainly. I was born in Scotland."

The Chief laughed loud. "Ha, ha," he said, "then Queenie England no take care a you. No send gunboat to shoot us all dead, if man a Tanaki come up and kill you."

At that Macglashin grew alarmed, and answered, "O, yes! The Queen of England would certainly avenge us." And he tried to explain the exact relation in which Scotchmen stood to the British crown, that they were just as much British subjects as Englishmen, entitled to precisely the same amount of protection. But the Chief couldn't be made to understand. The French skipper had evidently poisoned his mind against them. "Man a Tanaki don't want no Scotchman interfere with Chief when him go to sell him boy and him woman," the savage said angrily. "Tanaki belong a Queenie England. Queenie England no want Scotchman interfere with people in Tanaki. Scotchman better keep quiet in him house. Queenie England no mind Scotchman."

And no amount of reasoning produced any effect upon him.

The missionaries went to bed that evening with many misgivings. They felt that for the first time, so far as the natives were concerned, the powerful protection of the British flag was now practically withdrawn. They were alone, as strangers, among those excited black fellows.

At dead of night, while the two boys slept, a horrible din outside the mission-house awoke them. They looked out, and saw the red glare of torches outside. A frightful horde of Kanakas, naked save for their war-paint, drunk with the Frenchman's rum and armed with his Sniders, surrounded the frail building in a hideous mob of savagery. As Martin put his head out of the lattice a bullet came whizzing past. He withdrew it for a moment, terrified, and then looked out again. As he did so the other Scotch missionary appeared upon the veranda, half-dressed, and holding up his hand in dignified remonstrance, began in Kanaka with his gentle mild voice, "My friends, my dear friends, ..." Before he could get any further, the Chief stepped forward, and aiming a blow at his gray locks with a sacred native tomahawk, felled the peaceful old teacher senseless to the ground. Martin shuddered with horror. The old man lay weltering in a pool of his red gushing gore, while the savages danced in triumph over his prostrate body, or smeared themselves with great lines and circles of his warm heart-blood.

"Come on!" the Chief cried in Kanaka. "Kill all! Kill every one! They're taboo to our gods. Don't fear their gunboats. Queenie England won't trouble to protect a Scotchman!"

Then began a hideous orgy of wild lust and slaughter. The savages rushed on, drunk with blood and rum, and dragged out the wife and children of the other missionary, whom they brained upon the spot, before the terrified eyes of the trembling Macglashins. The trader Williams ran up just then, with his revolver in his hand, followed by two faithful black servants from a neighboring island; but the French skipper had been cunning enough there too. "Him a Welshman!" the savages cried. "Queenie England no care for him!" For indeed he happened to be born in Wales. And they shot him down as he came, before he could open fire upon them. Then they turned to massacre the Macglashins, the only remaining Europeans on the island.

But just at that moment a sudden idea seemed to strike the Chief. He cried out, "Stop!" The savages fell back and listened with eagerness to what was coming. Then the Chief shouted out again in Kanaka, "I have a thought. The gods have sent it to me. This is my thought. We have killed enough for tonight. Let us catch them alive and bind them. Next moon is the great feast of my father Taranaka. I have an idea, a divine idea. Let us keep them till that day, and then, in honor of the gods, let us roast them and eat them."

The whole assembly answered with a wild shout of delighted assent—"Taranaka! Taranaka! Our great dead Chief! In honor of Taranaka, let us roast them and eat them."

So they rushed wildly on upon the defenseless white family, bound them in rude cords of native make, and carried them off in triumph to Taranaka's temple tomb in the palm-grove.

And that was as much as we could allow the boys to tell us at a time, of their strange adventures. We were afraid of overtaxing their strength at first, and tried to confine their attention as much as possible to tinned meats and sea-biscuit soaked in condensed milk; though I'm bound to admit that as soon as they began to recover appetite a bit, they addressed themselves steadily and seriously to their food, with true British pluck and perseverance. In spite of the terrors from which they had just escaped, they did the fullest justice to Serang-Palo's cookery.

CHAPTER V

A BREAK-DOWN

Time went on, and the boys began to grow visibly fatter. It was Tuesday evening, and we hoped, putting on all steam as we were doing, to reach Tanaki by the small hours of Wednesday morning, in good season to relieve the four unhappy souls still, as we believed, detained there in captivity. We were strained on the very rack of excitement, indeed, with our efforts to arrive before the savages could take any further step; and the boys' anxiety for their parents' and their sister's safety had naturally communicated itself to us, as we listened to their story. Why, it was that very evening that Martin had told us the rest of his strange tale, how his father and mother, with his younger brother Calvin and his sister Miriam, had been confined by the savages in the grass-hut temple, while he and Jack were put to lie in an open out-house hard by, guarded only by a single half-intoxicated Kanaka. Well, in the middle of the night, those two brave boys had silently gnawed their ropes asunder, and creeping past their guard had stolen away to the beach in the desperate effort to escape in search of assistance. There, they luckily found the mission boat hauled down on the shore; and waiting only to take a can of water from the spring close by, and a bunch of half-ripe bananas from a garden on the harbor, they had put forth alone on their wild and adventurous voyage across the lone Pacific. I can tell you, it brought the tears to our eyes more than once, rough sailors as we were, to hear the strange story of their hopeless sail, and it made our blood boil to learn how these ungrateful savages had repaid the earnest and devoted life-labor of the unhappy missionaries.

"No wonder him hungry," that young monkey Nassaline said, with profound condolence, "if him don't hab nuffin to eat for ten day long but unripe banana." Anything that concerned the human stomach always touched a most tender and responsive chord in Nassaline's sympathies.

At eight bells when my watch was up, I went off for a quiet snooze to my cabin. I knew I should be wanted for hot work about three in the morning, for I didn't expect to effect the rescue without a hard fight for it; so I thought it best to get what sleep I could before arriving at the islands. So I lay in my berth, with my eyes shut, and a thin sheet spread over me (for it was broiling hot tropical weather), and I was just beginning to doze off in comfort, when suddenly I felt something move under me like a young earthquake. Next minute I was jolted clean out of my bed, with such a jerk that I thought at first we were all going to sleep on the bed of the ocean.

"Halloo," I cried out to Jim up atop, rushing out of my cabin. "What's up? Anything wrong? What's happened?"

"Grazed a reef, I guess," Jim shouted back, calmly. "No land in sight, but shoal water and breakers ahead. We seem to be in danger."

Cool chap, Jim, under no matter what circumstances. But this looked serious. In a second I was up, and peering out over the bows into the dark black water. The Albatross had slowed, and was reversing engines. All round us we could see great heaving breakers.

"No land hereabouts," Jim sung out, consulting the chart once more. "We ought to be at least five miles to suth'ard of the Great Caycos Band Reef."

As he spoke, I saw Martin's white face appearing suddenly at the top of the companion-ladder. He flung up his hands in an agony of despair. "Oh, how terrible!" the poor lad blurted out in his misery. "I ought to have remembered! I ought to have told you! Father says the charts hereabouts are all many miles wrong in their bearings. The Caycos Reef lies six or seven knots south by west of the point it's marked at!"

In a ferment of anxiety I turned up our other Sydney charts at once to test his statement. Sure enough there was a discrepancy, a considerable discrepancy, both in latitude and longitude, between the two maps. At the margin of one I read this vague and uncomfortable note—"These islands are reported by certain navigators to lie further south and west than here laid down, and have never been accurately surveyed by good authorities. Careful navigation by day alone is recommended to master mariners."

Jim looked at me, and I looked at Jim. What on earth could we do in such a fix as this? To go on in the dark, with unknown reefs before us, was to imperil the Albatross and all on board; to cast anchor where we stood and hold back till daylight was to risk not arriving in time to rescue the unfortunate missionary with his wife and family. I glanced at the boy's white face as he stood by the companion-ladder, and made up my mind at once. Come what might, I must push forward and save them.

"Slow engines," I called down the pipe, "and proceed half-speed till further orders. Jim, go for'ard, and keep a sharp eye on the breakers. As soon as we're clear, we'll steam ahead full pelt again, and risk going ashore sooner than leave these poor folks on the island to be cruelly massacred."

"Thank you," the boy said, with an ashy face, and lay down upon the deck, unmanned and trembling. His lips were as white, I give you my word, as this sheet of paper I'm this moment writing upon.

For a hundred yards or so we slowed, and went ahead without coming to any further stop; then suddenly, a sharp thud, a dull sound of grating, a thrill through the ship; and Jim, looking up from in front, with a cool face as usual, called out at the top of his voice, but with considerable annoyance, "By Jove, we're aground again!"

And so we were, this time with a vengeance.

"Back her," I called out, "back her hard, Jenkins!" and they backed her as hard as the engines could spurt; but nothing came of it. We were jammed on the reef about as tight as a ship could stick, and no power on earth could ever have got us off till the tide rose again.

Well, we tried our very hardest, reversing engines first, and then putting them forward again to see if we could run through it by main force; but it was all in vain. Aground we were, and aground we must remain till there was depth of water enough on the reef to float us.

Fortunately the tide was rising fast, and three hours more would see us out of our difficulties. Three hours was a very serious delay; but I calculated if we got off the reef by two in the morning, we should still have time to reach Tanaki pretty comfortably before seven. We must enter the harbor by daylight, no doubt, which would perhaps be dangerous; because when the savages saw us arrive, they might make haste to cut the white people's throats before we could get up to rescue them. But I thought it more likely they would try to save them, to prevent our opening fire upon them by way of punishment; so with what comfort we could, we stuck on upon the reef, and waited for the inevitable tide to come and float us.

Waiting for the tide is always slow business.

At about half-past one, however, the water began to deepen under the ship, and we could feel her rise and fall, bump, bump, bump, with each onslaught of the breakers. Now bumping on a reef isn't exactly wholesome for a ship's bottom, so I gave the word to Jenkins for the engines to go to work again; and presently, after two or three unsuccessful attempts, we got her safe off, by energetic reversing, and found to our great delight that the Albatross, like a tight little craft that she was, had sprung no leak, and was making no water. Her sound old timbers had just grazed the surface of that flat-topped reef without suffering any serious internal injury.

As soon as we were free, and had examined our hold, I shouted down once more, "Now forward, boys, as hard as you can go, and mind, Jenkins, you make her travel!"

To my immense surprise, instead of obeying my orders, the Albatross suddenly stood stock-still in the trough of a wave, drifting helplessly about like a log on the ocean.

"Now then," I shouted down again, half angry and half alarmed. "What are you doing there, Jenkins? Didn't you hear what I said? Stir your stumps, my friend! Double time, and forward!"

Imagine my horror when the engineer shouted back in a voice of blank dismay, "I can't, sir. She won't work. Don't answer to the valve. We've injured something in backing her off the reef there."

This was an awkward job. And at such a crisis, too! In a minute I was down in the engine-room myself, inspecting all the valves and bearings with lamp in hand, and with the closest scrutiny. Before long we had ascertained the extent of the injury. A piece of the engine was broken that would certainly take us six or eight hours to repair. And it was already two o'clock on the Wednesday morning!

But that wasn't all, either. Another serious difficulty beset us in our work. We were beating about in the angry sea off the Caycos Reef, with the breakers dashing in, and the surf running high. If we tried to mend the broken engine where we stood, we should infallibly be dashed to pieces on the dangerous shallows. You can't go to work like that on a lee shore, with no engine to fall back upon, and the wind blowing half a gale. The only thing possible for us was to hoist sail and make for the open sea to southward under all canvas. That was taking us further away from Tanaki, of course; but it was our one chance of getting our engine repaired in peace and quiet.

So we hoisted sail and stood out to sea once more, leaving the dim long line of surf gradually behind us on the lee, and beating by constant tacks against the wind, which had now veered to the southeast, and was blowing us straight on to the Caycos shallows.

By four o'clock we'd got so far out that we thought we might lie to a bit and take a few hands off navigating duty to assist the engineer in repairing his engine.

But it proved a much more difficult and lengthy task to retrieve the mischief than we had at first sight at all anticipated. The minutes went by with appalling rapidity. Five o'clock came, and the smith was only just getting his iron well hammered into shape. Six o'clock, and the engineer was still fitting the place it came from. Seven o'clock, something wrong, surely, with the ship's time! Before this hour I had hoped to be anchored off the harbor of Tanaki.

Seven o'clock on Wednesday morning; and by twelve at noon, so the boys assured us, the ovens would be made hot at Taranaka's tomb for those unfortunate prisoners on the remote island!

Oh, how frantically we worked for the next two hours! and how remorselessly everything seemed to turn against us! How is it that whenever one's in the greatest hurry all nature seems to conspire to defeat one's purpose? I won't attempt to explain to you all the petty mishaps and unfortunate failures that attended our efforts. It seemed as if iron, wood, and coal, all inanimate matter itself, was banded together to make our further approach to Tanaki impossible. By nine o'clock I knew the worst myself. The breakdown to the engine was far more serious than we had at first imagined. I felt sure that before noon at earliest, with all our skill and toil, we couldn't possibly repair it.

But I shrank from telling those two poor trembling lads that there was no hope now left of saving their parents.

Gradually, however, as the day wore on, they discovered it themselves, they saw that the golden opportunity had been lost for us. As each hour passed by they told us with ever redoubled horror what they knew must at that moment be passing on the island. Now the savages would be bringing their father out before the prison hut, and sacrificing him with their tomahawks by the hideous blood-stained altar of their great dead chieftain. Now their poor mother would be crouching on the ground, trying in vain to protect their helpless little brother. Now Miriam herself, little golden-haired, three-year-old, innocent Miriam, but at that last horror they broke down in tears, and could say no more. They could only sob and hide their faces in their hands with speechless agony at that unspeakable picture.

By noon we knew the worst must be over. They were at rest now, poor souls, from their month-long misery. The afternoon dragged on and we still worked hard on the mere chance of some respite which might enable us to rescue them. But we felt sure the end had come for all that. We worked away by the mere force of pure aimless energy. It distracted us from thinking of the awful events which we nevertheless in our hearts felt certain must have happened.

It was eight at night before we got the Albatross fairly under way again; and even then she lumbered slowly, slowly on, the engine being only somehow repaired, in the most clumsy fashion, till we could reach harbor once more, and quietly overhaul her.

So we steamed ahead, feebly and cautiously, all night long, keeping a sharp lookout for land across our bows, and with Martin on deck almost all the time, to aid us by his close personal knowledge of the island approaches.

Wednesday the tenth was over now. The terrible day had come and gone. We didn't doubt that the massacre was completed long before the clock struck one on Thursday morning.

CHAPTER VI

ON THE ISLAND

At Tanaki meanwhile, as we afterwards learned by inquiry among the islanders, things had been going on with the unhappy missionary very much as our worst fears had led us to expect. Though I wasn't there at the time to see for myself, I got to know what happened a little later almost as well as if I'd been on the spot; so I shall take the liberty once more, not being one of these book-making chaps, of telling my story my own way, and explaining how matters went in rough sailor fashion, without trying to let you know in detail how we found it all out till I come to explain the upshot of our present adventures.

Well, on the night when Martin and Jack stole away from the hut and got clear off on their venturesome journey in the mission boat, their father and mother, with little Calvin, who was eight years old, and Miriam, who was a pretty wee lassie of three, were heavily guarded by half a dozen desperate and drunken savages in the temple-tomb of the deceased Taranaka. It was a thatched native grass-house, with a bare mud floor, and a rough altar-slab raised high on the threshold, which covered the remains of the blood-thirsty old chieftain, the man who in his early youth had seen "Capitaney Cook" when he discovered the islands. The Melanesian natives, I ought to tell you, regard their dead ancestors as a sort of gods or guardian spirits, and frequently offer up food and drink at their graves as presents to appease them. Every morning gifts of taro, bread-fruit, and plantain were laid on the altar by Taranaka's tomb; and once every ten days a little square gin, mixed with cocoa-milk, was poured out upon the rude slab of unsculptured stone, that the dead chief's ghost might come to drink of it and be satisfied. Wednesday the tenth was the anniversary of Taranaka's death (he had been killed in a fight with some neighboring islanders, who fell out with him over the wreck of an American whaling vessel), and it was on that festival day that the chief proposed offering up the blood of our fellow-countrymen as an expiation to the shades of his departed relative.

Macglashin and his wife never even knew that the boys had escaped. If they had, those long days of suspense might have been even worse for them. They might have been looking forward with mad hope to some miracle of rescue such as that which the Albatross had so boldly planned, and which had been so cruelly interfered with by the breakdown of our machinery. As it was, the savages carefully kept from them all knowledge of their boys' escape. They never even breathed a hint of that desperate voyage. Every day, on the contrary, when they brought the unhappy missionary and his wife their daily rations of yam and banana, they taunted them with threats of what tortures the Chief had still in store for Jack and Martin. They were fatting them up, they said, for Taranaka to feed upon. On Taranaka's day they would be offered up as victims on the cannibal altar.

But the most terrible part of all the poor father and mother's sufferings was the fact that they couldn't keep the knowledge of that awful fate in store for them even from Calvin and pretty little Miriam. Macglashin's diary, which I read later on, was just heartrending about the children. Those helpless mites cowered all day long on the bare mud floor of that hideous temple, awaiting the horrible doom that the savages held out before them with the painful resignation of innocent childhood. They were too frightened to cry over it; too frightened to talk of it; they only crouched pale and terrified by their mother's side, and dragged out the long day in horrible apprehensions. They knew they must die, and they sat there watching for that inevitable sentence to be carried out with the stoical fortitude of utter childish helplessness. Well, there, I'm an old hand on the sea, you know, and I don't mind the dangers of the wind and waves for grown men and boys that can look after themselves, any more than most of you land-folks mind dodging about in the Strand at Charing Cross on a crowded afternoon in the London season; but I can't bear to talk or even to think of what those poor children suffered all those terrible days in the heathen tomb-house. There are things that make a man's blood run cold to speak about. That makes mine run cold: I can't dwell on it any longer; it's too ghastly to realize.

So there, the days went by, one after another; and Monday the eighth came, and Tuesday the ninth, and still no chance of escape or rescue. Up to the last moment, Macglashin hoped (as he says in the diary) that some miracle might occur to set them free, some interposition of Providence on their behalf to prevent the last misfortune from overtaking his poor pallid little Miriam. Perhaps the mission ship, that went her rounds twice a year, might happen to put in, out of due season, with some special message or under stress of weather; or perhaps some whaling vessel or some English gunboat might arrive in the nick of time in the little harbor of Tanaki. But when Tuesday evening came, and no help had arrived, the unhappy man's heart sank within him. He gave up that last wild hope of a rescue at the eleventh hour, and addressed himself to die with what courage he could muster.

Ah yes, to die one's self is all easy enough; nobody worth his salt minds that; but to see one's wife and children murdered before one's eyes, there, I'm a rough sort of sailor-body, as I said before, but you must excuse my breaking off. I haven't got the strength to hold my pen and write about it. Why, I've a boy of my own at school at Sydney, and my Mary's in England, bless her little heart! at a lady's college they call it nowadays; and I know what it means; I know what it means, gentlemen. I'd no more expose those two dear children in the places I've been among the islands myself, than, well, than I'd send them to sea alone in a cock-boat. And my heart just bleeds for that poor father at Tanaki, when I read his diary over again, though I haven't got the skill to put it all down in words at full length as one of those fellows would do that write for the newspapers.

However, on Tuesday night, neither Macglashin himself nor Mrs. Macglashin could get a wink of sleep, as you may easily imagine. They sat up in the temple, with their backs against the wall, and relays of black fellows, armed with Sniders, and smeared with red paint, watching them closely all the while, to see they didn't escape or try to do away with themselves. But Calvin fell asleep out of pure fatigue on his mother's lap, and Miriam, poor little soul, lay against her father's shoulder, dozing as peacefully as ever she dozed in her own small cot at the mission-house, where she was born. Once the thought came into her father's mind, oughtn't he to twist his handkerchief round her soft little throat, as she lay there all unconscious in his circling arms, to save her from the tender mercies of those cruel black savages? How could he tell what torments they might inflict upon her? Wasn't it better she should be spared all that horror of fear? Wasn't it better she should just sleep away her dear little life without ever knowing it, till she woke next morning in a happier and a brighter country? But in another minute his heart recoiled from the terrible thought. While there was still one chance of safety he must let things take their course. Perhaps even those black monsters might have pity at the last on that one ewe lamb. Perhaps they might spare his Miriam's life, and make her over to the mission-ship when it next arrived on its rounds at the island.

All that night long the savages, for their part, were holding a sing-sing, as they call it, close by, and the hideous noise of their heathenish revels could be distinctly heard by the watchers in the temple. They danced to the music of their hollow drums, while the shells upon their ankles resounded in unison. At times the echo of horrible laughter fell harsh upon the ear. The natives, covered with red feathers and smeared with blood, were keeping high festival, as is their horrid custom. And as the long hours wore away, the din of their revelry became more wild in their orgies each moment.

Morning dawned at last, the morning of Wednesday the tenth, when that awful deed of bloodshed was to be done before the open eye of heaven; and with the first streak of light the poor children awoke and gazed around them blankly at their temple prison. The black watchers brought them yam and mammee-apples once more, but they couldn't eat; they sat bewildered and mute, with their hands clasped in their parents' palms, waiting for the end, and too dazed and terrified almost to know what was passing.

About six o'clock the Chief came down to the temple, with bloodshot eyes and tottering feet, attended by half a dozen naked black followers. They had all been drinking the greater part of the night at the sing-sing, for the Frenchmen had left plenty of square gin behind; and they rollicked in the cruel good-humor of the born savage.

"How do, Macglashin?" the Chief inquired with a hateful leer. "How do, white woman? Taranaka day come at last. How you like him this morning? What for you no tell man a Tanaki sooner you don't know Englishman? Ha! ha! dat true; so him see. Queenie England no care for Scotchman."

"If you dare to touch a hair of our heads," Macglashin cried in his despair, rising up and facing the savage angrily, "sooner or later, I tell you, the Queen of England will hear of it, and she'll send a gunboat to punish you for our death, and her sailors'll shoot you all down for your part in this murder."

The Chief laughed, a wild, horrible, barbaric laugh. "Ha! ha!" he answered. "Dat all very fine for try frighten me. But man a oui-oui tell me you no true Englishman. You speakee English, but you Scotchman born. All samee American. Queenie England no care for American, no care for Scotch; no send her gunboat for look after Scotchman. Man a Tanaki go for eat you to-day, for do honor to ghost a Taranaka."

Macglashin saw that words would produce no effect upon the tipsy and excited wretch; he must make up his mind for the worst. There was no help for it.

"At least," he cried, "Chief, you'll let us say good-by to our boys before we die? You'll bring them in for their mother and me to take our last farewell of them?"

The Chief shook his head and made a hideous grimace. "No say good-by to boys," he said, with horrible glee. "Man a Tanaki kill pig all night; kill Scotchman in morning. Kill baby first; then boy; then mother. Last of all, kill you yourself, Macglashin. Taranaka very much love white man's blood. Great day to-day for feast for Taranaka." And he went off again, grinning in hideous buffoonery, while Macglashin's soul seethed in speechless indignation.

For half an hour more they were left undisturbed. Then the Chief appeared at the door once more, and beckoning with his long black forefinger, called to the missionary—

"Come out, Macglashin!"

The unhappy man strode out with little Miriam half-fainting in his arms.

"Come out, white woman!" the savage cried once more.

The pale mother, almost unable to totter with terror, made her way to the door, with Calvin's fingers intertwined in her own.

"Now, white people, we going to shoot you," the savage continued, unabashed. "You make too much trouble for man a Tanaki. Interfere too much with man who sell him boy or him woman. Me don't going to kill you with axe, like Taranaka kill first missionary that come a Tanaki. Man a oui-oui sell me plenty Snider. Man a Tanaki want to try him shooting-irons. Set you up to run, and then go fire at you."

At the word he nodded, and four stalwart savages caught Macglashin in their arms and held him to a line drawn lightly in the dust by the Chief's stick. At the same moment four others caught his unhappy wife, and dragged her, half senseless, to the self-same line. The two children were ranged by their sides, pale and white with terror. Then the Chief walked forward, and drew another line some forty yards in front of them with his stick again. "When Chief call 'go,'" he called out, "man a Tanaki let go missionary, and boy, and white woman. Missionary run till him reach dis line. Man a Tanaki no shoot till missionary pass dis line. Den man a Tanaki fire; missionary run; man a Tanaki run after missionary to kill him. Whoever shoot missionary or white woman first, give him body up in temple to Taranaka."

As he spoke, the savages ranged themselves behind, Sniders in hand. The Chief placed himself in order at their head on the right. Then he called out in Kanaka, "When I give the word, 'one, two, three'—loose them! When I give the word Fire! off with your rifles at them."

There was a deadly pause. All was still as death. Then the Chief cried aloud, "One—two—three—loose them!" and the savages loosed the poor terrified Europeans.

Even in that supreme moment of agony and doubt, however, one thought kept rising ever in the father's and mother's heart. What had become of Jack and Martin?

CHAPTER VII

ERRORS EXCEPTED

It was Thursday the eleventh, in the small hours of the morning. The Albatross was lumbering along as best she might with her broken engine, and we were nearing the line of 180°. We weren't making much way, however, for the speed was low; and we hadn't so much reason for hurrying now, for we felt almost hopeless of being in time to prevent the threatened massacre. Our people, we feared, had long since fallen victims to the superstition and bloodthirstiness of the ungrateful savages.

I was asleep in my berth after the fatigues of the day, and was dreaming of my dear little girl in England; when suddenly I felt a clammy cold hand laid upon my own outside the coverlet, and waking with a start, I saw Martin Luther standing pale and white in his blue shirt and trousers before me. I knew at once by his face something fresh had turned up.

"Goodness gracious, boy," I exclaimed, "what on earth's the matter now?"

"Captain Braithwaite," he answered with very solemn seriousness, "I've been counting the days over and over again, and I'm quite sure there's a mistake somewhere. We've got a day wrong in our reckoning, I'm certain. I've counted up each day and night a hundred times over since we left Tanaki in the boat, Jack and I, and I feel confident you're twenty-four hours out in your reckoning. Yesterday wasn't Wednesday the tenth at all. It was Tuesday the ninth, and we may yet reach Tanaki in time to save them."

"No, no, my boy," I answered, "you're wrong; you're wrong. Your natural anxiety about your father's fate has upset your calculations. To-day's the eleventh; yesterday was the tenth. Till we get to the meridian of 180°"—and then, with a start, I broke off suddenly.

"What's the matter?" Martin cried, for he saw at once I was faltering and hesitating. "Ah, you see I was right now. You see this morning's the tenth, don't you?"

In a moment the truth flashed across me with a burst. I saw it all; the only wonder was how on earth I had failed so long to perceive it. I seized the poor lad's hand in a fervor of delight, relief and exultation.

"Martin," I cried, overjoyed, "we are both of us right in our own way of reckoning. This morning's the eleventh on board the Albatross here, but it's the tenth, I don't doubt, in your island at Tanaki!"

"What do you mean?" he cried, astonished, and gazing at me as if he thought me rather more than half-mad. "How on earth can it be Thursday here, while it's Wednesday at Tanaki?"

"Hold on a bit, youngster," said I, jumping out of my cabin, "till I've consulted the chart and made quite sure about it. Let me see. Here we are. Duke of Cumberland's Islands, 179° west. Hooray! Hooray!" I waved the chart round my head in triumph. "Jim, Jim!" I shouted out, rushing up the companion-ladder in my night-shirt as I stood; "here's a hope indeed! Here's splendid news. Put on all steam at once and we may save them yet. Tanaki's the other side of 180!"

Jim looked at me in astonishment.

"Why, what on earth do you mean, Julian?" he asked. "What on earth has that to do with our chance of saving them?"

"Jim," I cried once more, hardly knowing how to contain myself with excitement and reaction; "was there ever such a precious pair of fools in the world before as you and me, my good fellow? It's Wednesday morning in Tanaki, man! It's Wednesday in Tanaki! Tanaki's the other side of 180!"

As I said the words, Jim jumped at me like a wild creature and grasped my hand hard. Then he caught Martin in his arms and hugged him as tight as if he'd been his own father. After that he threw his cap up in the air and shouted aloud with delight. And when he'd quite finished all those remarkable performances, he looked hard into my face and burst out laughing.

"Well, upon my soul, Julian," he said, "for a couple of seasoned old Pacific travelers, I do agree with you that a pair of bigger fools and stupider dolts than you and I never sailed the ocean!"

"If it had been our first voyage across now," I said to Jim, feeling thoroughly ashamed of myself for my silly mistake, "there might have been some excuse for us!"

"Or if the boy hadn't told us there was a discrepancy in the accounts the very first day he ever came aboard," he added solemnly.

"But as it is," I went on, "such a scholar's mate, such a beginner's blunder as this is for two seafaring men, why, it's absolutely inexcusable!"

"Absolutely inexcusable!" Jim repeated, penitently.

"But if we clap on all steam we may get there yet on Wednesday morning," I continued, consulting my watch.

"By three or four o'clock on Wednesday morning," Jim echoed, examining the chart once more, and carefully noting the ship's position. "Why, it's Wednesday now, Julian. We've crossed 180°."

"But what day was yesterday?" Martin asked, all trembling.

"Why, yesterday," I answered, "was Wednesday the tenth, my boy; but to-day is Wednesday the tenth also. It comes twice over at this longitude. We've gained a day; that's the long and the short of it. We ought to have known it, my brother and I, who are such old hands at cruising in and out of the islands; but our anxiety and distress made us clean forget it."

"How does that come about?" Martin asked bewildered, his lips white as death.

"Just like this," said I. "Sailing one way, you see, from England, you sail with the sun; and sailing the other way, you sail against it. In one direction you keep gaining time, and in the other you lose it."

"The meridian of 180° is the particular place where the two modes of reckoning reach their climax," I hastened to add. "So, when you get to 180°, sailing west, you lose a day, and Saturday's followed right off by Monday. But sailing east, you gain a day, and have two Sundays running, or whatever else the day may be when you happen to get there. Now, we're going in the right direction for gaining a day; and so, though yesterday was Wednesday the tenth the other side of 180°, to-day's Wednesday the tenth, don't you see, this side of it? And as Tanaki's this side, your people must always have reckoned by the American day, so to speak, while we've reckoned all along by the Australian one. It's this morning those savages threatened to kill your father and mother, and if we make a good run, we shall still perhaps be in time to save them."

As I spoke, the boy's knees trembled under him with excitement. He staggered so that he caught at a rope for support. He was too much in earnest to cry, but the tears stood still in his eyes without falling.

"Oh! I hope to Heaven we'll be in time," he answered. "We may save them! We may save them!"

I went below and turned in once more for a little sleep, for I knew I should be wanted later in the morning; and having fortunately the true sailor's habit in that matter of dozing off whenever occasion occurred, I was soon snoring away again most comfortably on my pillow. At half-past three, Tom Blake came down once more to wake me.

"Land in sight, sir," he said, "on our starboard bow, and this young fellow Martin says he makes it out to be the north point of Tanaki."

In a minute I was on deck again, and peering at the dim land through the gray mist of morning, the same gray mist through which, as we afterwards learned, the poor creatures in the heathen temple saw the dawn break of the day that was to end their earthly troubles. It was Tanaki, no doubt, for Martin was quite sure he could recognize the headlands and the barrier reef. Our only question now was how next to proceed. We held a brief little council of war on deck, with Martin as our chief adviser on the local situation.

From what he told us, I came rapidly to the conclusion that it would be useless to attempt an open entrance into the little harbor of Makilolo, where the Chief had his hut, and where the mission-people, as we believed, were still confined in the temple. To do so would only be to arouse the anger of the savages beforehand; and unless we could get them well between a cross fire, and so effectually prevent any further outrage, we feared they might massacre the unhappy people in their hands the moment we hove in sight to enter the harbor. But here our friend Martin's local knowledge of the archipelago helped us out of our difficulty. He could pilot us, he said, to a retired bay at the back of the island, by the east side, where we could land a small party in boats, well armed with Sniders and our Winchester repeater; and Jack, who had slept all night, and was therefore the fresher of the two, would show us a path through the thick tropical underbrush by which we could approach the village from the rear, while the Albatross ran round again with the remainder of the crew, and brought our brass thirty-pounder to bear upon the savages from the open harbor.

This plan was at once received with universal approbation, and we proceeded forthwith to put it into execution.

Steering cautiously round the island, under cover of the mist, and fortunately unperceived by the assembled natives, who were too much occupied with their sing-sing to be engaged in scanning the offing, we reached at last the little retired bay of which Martin had spoken, and got ready our boat to land our military party. It was ticklish work, for we could afford to land only ten, all told, with Jack for our guide; but each man was armed with a good rifle and ammunition, and the habit of discipline made our little band, we believed, more than a match for those untutored savages. Nassaline, also, joined the military party, while seven men were left as a naval reserve. Silently and cautiously we landed on the white sandy beach, and turned with Jack into the thick tangled brake of tropical brushwood.

Meanwhile, my brother Jim, with Martin to guide him, undertook to take the Albatross round to the regular harbor; for Martin fortunately knew every twist and turn of those tortuous reef-channels, having been accustomed to navigate them from his childhood upwards, both in the mission-boat and in the native canoes which frequently put to sea for the bêche-de-mer fishery.

Our plan of action, as arranged beforehand, was for the military party to wait about in the woods at the back of the village till the Albatross hove in sight off the mouth of the harbor. Then, the moment she appeared, she was to fire a blank shot towards the Chief's hut with her thirty-pounder; and at the same moment, we of the surprise party were to fall upon the savages, and before they could recover from their first surprise, demand the instant restitution of the missionary and his family.

Everything depended now upon the two boys. If Jack failed to show us the path aright, if Martin drove the Albatross upon reef or rock, all would be up with us, and the savages would massacre our whole party in cold blood, as they proposed to do with Macglashin and his little ones. I trembled to think on how slender a thread those four precious human lives depended. After all, they were but lads, mere children almost, and the rash confidence of youth might easily deceive them. But I decided, none the less, to trust to their instincts and their keen affection for their friends to see us through in our need. If that wouldn't lead us right, I felt sure in my own soul no human aid could possibly save the unhappy prisoners.

CHAPTER VIII

HOT WORK

Jack led us from the beach over the white coral sand straight up to the wood, and after looking about for a while to make sure of his bearings among the huge fallen logs, hit at last upon a faint trail that led straggling through the forest, a trail scarcely worn into the semblance of a path by the bare feet of naked savages. Following his guidance, we plunged at once, with some doubtful misgivings, into the deep gloom of the woodland, and found ourselves immediately in a genuine equatorial thicket, where mouldering trunks of palms encumbered the vague path, and great rope-like lianas hung down in loops from the trees overhead, to block our way at every second step through that fatiguing underbrush. The day was warm, even as we travelers who know the world judge warmth in the tropical South Pacific; and the moist heat of that basking, swampy lowland, all laden with miasma from the decaying leaves, seemed to oppress us with its deadly effluvia and its enervating softness at every yard we went through the jungle. Moreover, we had to carry our arms and ammunition among that tangled brake; and as our rifles kept catching continually in the creepers that drooped in festoons from the branches, while our feet got simultaneously entangled in the roots and trailing stems that straggled underfoot, you can easily imagine for yourself that ours was indeed no pleasant journey. However, we persevered with dogged English perseverance; the sailors tramped on and wiped their foreheads with their sleeves from time to time; while poor Jack marched bravely at our head with an indomitable pluck which reflected the highest credit on Mr. Macglashin's training.

The only one who seemed to make light of the toil was our black boy, Nassaline.

We went single file, of course, along the narrow trail, which every here and there divided to right or left in the midst of the brake with most puzzling complexity. At every such division or fork in the track, Jack halted for a moment and cast his eye dubiously to one side and the other, at last selecting the trail that seemed best to him. Nassaline, too, helped us not a little by his savage instinct for finding his way through trackless jungle. For my own part, I could never have believed any road on earth could possibly be so tortuous; and at last, at the end of the twenty-fifth turn or thereabouts, I ventured to say in a very low voice (for we were stealing along in dead silence), "Why, Jack, I believe you're leading us round and round in a circle, and you'll bring us out again in the end at the very same bay where we first landed!"

"Hush!" Jack answered, with one finger on his lip. "We're drawing near the outskirts of the village now. You must be very quiet. I can just see the grass roof of Taranaka's temple peeping above the brushwood to the right. In three minutes more we shall be out in the open."

And sure enough he told the truth. Almost as he ceased speaking, the noise of savage voices fell full upon my ear from the village in front, and I could hear the natives, in their hideous corroboree, beating hard upon their hollow drums of stretched skin, and shouting in the dance to their drunken comrades.

It was a ghastly noise, but it did our hearts good just then to hear it.

I could almost have clapped my hand upon Jack's back and given him three cheers for his gallant guidance when we saw the village plot opening up in front of us, and the naked savages, in their war-paint and feathers, guarding the door of Taranaka's temple. But the necessity for caution compelled me to preserve a solemn silence. So we crouched as still as mice behind a clumpy thicket of close-leaved tiro bushes, and peeped out from our ambush through the dense foliage to keep an eye upon the scene till the Albatross hove into sight in the harbor.

"My father and my mother must still be there," Jack whispered under his breath, but in a deep tone of relief. "The Tanaki men are guarding them exactly as they did when Martin and I left the island. I almost think I can see Miriam's head through the open door. We shall be in time still to deliver them from these bloodthirsty wretches."

"In what direction must we look for the Albatross?" I whispered back. "Will she come in from the south there?"

"O, no!" Jack answered in a very low voice. "That's an island to the right, a little rocky island that guards the harbor. There's deep water close in by the shore that side. Martin 'll try to bring her in the northern way, so that the natives mayn't see her till she's close upon the village. It's a difficult channel to the north, all full of reefs and sunken rocks; but I think he understands it, he's swam in it so often. We won't see her at all till she's right in the harbor and just opposite the temple."

We were dying of thirst now, and longing for drink, but could get nothing to quench our drought. "What I would give," I muttered to Tom Blake, "for a drink of water!"

"If Captain want water," Nassaline answered, "me soon get him some." And he made a gash with his knife in the stem of a sort of gourd that climbed over the bushes, from which there slowly oozed and trickled out a sort of gummy juice that relieved to some degree our oppressive sensations. All the men began at once cutting and chewing it, with considerable satisfaction. It wasn't as good as a glass of British beer, I will freely admit; but still, it was better than nothing, any way.

By this time it was nearly half-past six, and we watched eagerly to see what action the natives would take as soon as they finished their night-long sing-sing. Lying flat on the ground, with our rifles ready at hand, and our heads just raised to look out among the foliage, we kept observing their movements cautiously through the thick brushwood.

At a quarter to seven we saw some bustle and commotion setting in on a sudden in front of the temple; and presently a tall and sinister-looking native, who, Jack whispered to me, was the Chief of Tanaki, came up from the village, where the sing-sing had taken place, and stood by the door of the thatched grass-house. We could distinctly hear him call the missionary to come out in pigeon English; and next moment our unfortunate countryman staggered forth, with his little daughter half fainting in his arms, and stood out in the bare space between the tomb of Taranaka and the spot where we were lying.

Oh! how I longed to take a shot at that miscreant black fellow.

At sight of his father, worn with fatigue and pale with the terror of that agonizing moment, Jack almost cried aloud in his mingled joy and apprehension; but I clapped my hand on his mouth and kept him still for the moment. "Not a sound, my boy, not a sound," I whispered low, "till the time comes for firing!"

"Shall we give it them hot now?" Tom Blake inquired low at my ear next moment. But I waved him aside cautiously.

"Not yet," I answered, "unless the worst comes to the worst, and we see our people in pressing and immediate danger; we'd better do nothing till the Albatross heaves in sight. Her gun will frighten them. To fire now would be to expose ourselves and our friends there to unnecessary danger."

"All right, sir," Tom murmured low in reply. "You know best, of course. But I must say, it'd do my 'eart good to up an' pepper 'em!"

"Come out, white woman!" we heard the Chief say next with insolent familiarity; and Mrs. Macglashin stepped out, a deplorable figure, with her boy's hand twined in hers, and her white lips twitching with horror for her little ones. It made one's blood boil so to see it that we could hardly resist the temptation as we looked to fire at all hazards, and let them know good friends were even now close at hand to help and deliver them.

"Whether the Albatross heaves in sight or not," I whispered to Tom Blake, "we must fire at them soon, within five minutes, and sell our lives as dearly as we can. I can't stand this much longer. It's too terrible a strain. Come what may, I must give the word and at them!"

"Quite right, sir," says Tom. "What's the use of delaying?"

And, indeed, I began to be terribly afraid by this time there was something very wrong indeed somewhere. Could Martin have missed his way among those difficult shoals, and run our trusty vessel helplessly on the rocks and reefs? It looked very like it. They were certainly overdue; for even at the present crippled rate of speed, the good old Albatross had had plenty of time, I judged, to round the point and get back safe again into the deep water of the harbor. If she failed in this our hour of need, the natives would surround us and cut us to pieces in a mass, for our best reliance was in our solid brass thirty-pounder. I began to tremble in my shoes for some time for the possible upshot. Over and over again I glanced eagerly towards the point for that longed-for white nose of hers to appear round the corner.

At last, unable to restrain my curiosity any longer, I rose to my feet and peered across the bushes. As I did so, I saw the savages seize Macglashin in their arms, and range the four poor fugitives in a line together. My blood curdled. The Chief and the ten savages with the Sniders stood in a row, half fronting us where we lay. Macglashin and his wife were fortunately out of line of fire for our rifles. "Now, we can delay no longer," I cried. "He means murder. The moment the black fellow gives the word of command, fire at once upon him and his men, boys. Take steady aim. No matter what comes. Let the poor souls have a run for their lives, any way."

As I spoke, the Chief uttered in Kanaka the native words for "One, two, three," with loud drunken laughter.

At the sound of the Chief's voice, the savages loosed the four wretched Europeans. At the very same sound we all fired simultaneously, and six of the black monsters fell writhing on the ground, while the Chief and the four others, taken completely by surprise, dropped their rifles in their supreme astonishment.

"Forward, boys, and secure them!" I cried, dashing out into the open, and waving my hat to the astounded missionary. "Here we are, sir. Run this way! We're friends. We've come to your rescue. Catch the Chief at once, lads; and hooray for the Albatross!"

For just as I spoke, to my joy and relief, her good white nose showed at last round the point; and next instant, the boom! boom! of her jolly brass thirty-pounder, fired in the very nick of time, completed the discomfiture of the astonished savages.

Before they knew where they were, they found themselves hemmed in between a raking cross-fire from our Sniders on one side, and the heavy gun of the Albatross on the other. The tables were now completely turned. We charged at them, running. Macglashin, seizing the situation at a glance, caught up one of the rifles belonging to the wounded men, which had been flung upon the ground, and, hardly yet realizing his miraculous escape, joined our little party as an armed recruit with surprising alacrity. For the next ten minutes there was a terrible scene of noise and confusion. The blacks advanced upon us, swarming up from the village like bees or wasps, and it was only by a hand-to-hand fight with our bayonets, for we had fortunately brought them in case of close quarters, that we kept our dusky enemy at bay. At last, however, after a smart hand-to-hand contest, we secured the Chief, and tied him safely with the rope he had loosed from Macglashin. Then we seized the remaining Sniders that lay upon the ground, while the men of the village, drunk and stupefied, began to fall back a little and molest us from a distance.

"Now, put the lady and children in the center, boys," I cried, at the top of my voice, "and let the Chief march along with us as a hostage. Down to the shore, while the Albatross boat puts out to save us!" Then I turned to the savages, and called out in English, "If any one of you dares to fire at us, I give you fair warning, we shoot your Chief! Hold off there, all of you!"

To my great delight, Nassaline, standing forward as I spoke, translated my words to them into their own tongue, and waving them back with his hands made a little alley for us through the midst to regain the shore by. Smart boy, Nassaline!

After a moment, however, the natives once more began to crowd round us, as we started to march, in very threatening attitudes, with their Sniders and hatchets. At one time I almost thought they would overpower us; but just then Jim, who was watching the proceedings with his glass from the deck of the Albatross, and saw exactly how matters stood, created a judicious diversion at the exact right moment by firing a little grape-shot plump into the heart of the grass huts of the village, and bowling over a roof or two before the very eyes of the astonished savages. They fell back at once, and began to make signs of desiring a parley. So we halted on the spot, with the lady and children still carefully guarded, and held up our handkerchiefs in sign of truce. Then Nassaline, aided by our sailor who understood the Kanaka language, began to palaver with them. He told them in plain and simple terms we must first be allowed to take the lady and children in safety to the Albatross, and that we would afterwards come back to treat at greater length with their head men as to the Chief's safety. To this, after some demur, the black fellows assented; and we beckoned to Jim accordingly by a preconcerted sign to send the boat ashore to us, to fetch off the fugitives. At the same time we retreated in military order, in a small hollow square, to the beach, still taking good care to protect in the midst our terrified non-combatants.

As for the Chief, he marched before us, with his hands tied, and his feet free, led by a rope, the ends of which I held myself, with the aid of two of my sailors. A more ridiculously crestfallen or disappointed creature than that drunken and conquered savage at that particular moment it has never yet been my fate to light upon.

We reached the beach in safety, and sent Mrs. Macglashin and the children aboard, with Jack to accompany them. Then we turned to parley with the discomfited savages. Jim kept the thirty-pounder well pointed in their direction, with ostentatious precision, and we made them hold off along the beach at a convenient distance, where he could rake them in security, while we ourselves retained the Chief in our hands, with a pistol at his head, as a gentle reminder that we meant to stand no nonsense.

After a few minutes' parley, conducted chiefly by our Kanaka-speaking sailor, with an occasional explanation put in by our assistant-interpreter, Nassaline, we arrived at an understanding, in accordance with which we were to return them their Chief for the time being, on consideration of their bringing us down to the beach all the Macglashins' goods, and making restitution for the sack of the mission-house in dried cocoa-nut, the sole wealth of the island. Those were the terms for the immediate present, as a mere personal matter: for the rest, we gave the Chief clearly to understand that we intended to sail straight away with all our guests for Fiji, there to lay our complaint of his conduct before the British High Commissioner in the South Pacific. We would then charge him with murder and attempted cannibalism, and with stirring up his people to massacre the other missionary, and the trader Freeman. We would endeavor to get a gunboat sent to the spot, to make official inquiry into the nature of the disturbances, and to demand satisfaction on the part of the relations of the murdered men. Finally, we would also lay before the Commissioner the conduct of the French labor-vessel, and her kidnaping skipper, who had instigated the savages to their dastardly attack, and whom I was strongly inclined to identify with the captain from whose grip we had rescued our friend Nassaline. We gave the Chief to understand, therefore, that he must by no means consider himself as scot free, merely because we let him go unhurt till trial could be instituted by the proper authorities. He must answer hereafter for his high crimes and misdemeanors to the Queen's representative.

To all of which the penitent savage merely answered with a sigh:

"Me make mistake. Kill missionary by accident. Man a oui-oui tell me Queenie England no care for Scotchman, an' me too much believe him. Now Captain tell me Queenie send gunboat for eat me up, and kill all my people. No listen any more to man a oui-oui."

And then we put off in triumph to the Albatross. The family meeting that ensued on board when Macglashin stood once more upon a British deck with his wife and children, I won't attempt, rough sailor as I am, to describe: I don't believe even the special correspondent of a morning paper could do full justice to it. To see those two lads, too, catch their pretty little sister once more in their arms, and cover her with kisses, while she clung to their necks and cried and laughed alternately, was a sight to do a man's heart good for another twelvemonth. And as we sat that same evening round the cabin-table (where our Malay cook had performed wonders of culinary art for the occasion), and drank healths all round to everybody concerned in this remarkable rescue, the toast that was received with the profoundest acclamations from every soul on board, was that of the two brave boys whose courage and skill had guided us at last, as if by a miracle, to the recovery of all that was nearest and dearest to them.

Indeed, if Martin and Jack don't get the Victoria Cross when we return to England, I shall have even a lower opinion than ever before of her Majesty's confidential political advisers of all creeds or parties.

Grant Allen – A Short Biography

Charles Grant Blairfindie Allen was born on February 24th, 1848 at Alwington, near Kingston, Canada West (now part of Ontario). He was the second son of the Rev. Joseph Antisell Allen, a Protestant minister from Dublin, Ireland and Catharine Ann Grant, the daughter of the fifth Baron of Longueuil.

Grant was educated at home until he was thirteen at which time the family moved, initially to the United States, then France and finally settling in the United Kingdom.

Whilst growing up the family background was obviously religious but Grant developed his own views on life and the world and turned to agnosticism and socialism.

He was educated at King Edward's School in Birmingham and Merton College in Oxford. After graduating, Grant studied in France and also taught at Brighton College. By 1870, still only in his mid-twenties, he became a professor at Queen's College, a black college in Jamaica.

Whilst in Jamaica Grant met and married his first wife Ellen Jerrard in 1873 and they produced a son five years later; Jerrard Grant Allen, who grew up to become a theatrical agent/manager.

In 1876 Grant and his family left Jamaica to return to England with both the talent and ambition to become a writer.

He quickly turned to writing essays, gaining a reputation for his work on science and literary works. An early article, 'Note-Deafness' a description of what is now called amusia, was published in 1878 in the learned journal Mind and was cited approvingly by Oliver Sacks very recently.

From essays in magazines and journals he now turned to books, initially on scientific subjects. These include Physiological Æsthetics 1877 and Flowers and Their Pedigrees 1886.

His first major influence was associationist psychology, as then expounded by Alexander Bain and Herbert Spencer, the latter is often considered the most important individual in the transition from associationist psychology to Darwinian functionalism. In Grant's many articles on flowers and perception in insects, Darwinian arguments now replaced the old Spencerian terms.

On a personal level, a long friendship that started when Grant met Herbert Spencer on his return from Jamaica, turned eventually to one of unease over its long course. Grant was to write a critical and revealing biographical article on Spencer that was published after Spencer was dead.

In the early 1880's Grant began to assist Sir W. W. Hunter in his Gazeteer of India. It is at this time that Grant now turned his full attention away from the factual and towards the world of imagination and fiction.

Between this shift to fiction in 1884 and his death fifteen years later Grant was to write about 30 novels.

Many were adventure novels which were very common in the late Victorian period as writers turned their literary talents to the voracious appetites of the weekly or monthly serial magazines.

Some however were to cause quite a stir. For instance in 1895 Grant took the subject of children born out of wedlock as his subject matter. The result was The Woman Who Did, that suggested, indeed pushed, for its time, certain quite startling views on marriage and related areas. In keeping with his then glowing reputation it became a bestseller despite it being seemingly at odds with society's unease at its provocative subject matter.

Interestingly Grant wrote novels under female pseudonyms. One of these was the short novel The Type-writer Girl, which he wrote under the name Olive Pratt Rayner.

Another work, The Evolution of the Idea of God 1897, propounding a theory of religion on heterodox lines, has the disadvantage of endeavoring to explain everything by one theory. This "ghost theory" was often seen as a derivative of Herbert Spencer's theory. However, at the time, it was well known and brief references to it can be found in a review by Marcel Mauss, Durkheim's nephew, in the articles of William James and in the works of Sigmund Freud. The young G. K. Chesterton wrote on what he considered the flawed premise of the idea, arguing that the idea of God preceded human mythologies, rather than developing from them. Chesterton said of Grant Allen's book on the evolution of the idea of God "it would be much more interesting if God wrote a book on the evolution of the idea of Grant Allen".

From this and other instances, it can be seen that his work was in debate and whether agreed with or not could always ensure a lively discussion.

Grant also helped to pioneer science fiction, with the 1895 novel The British Barbarians. This book, was published at about the same time as H. G. Wells was to publish The Time Machine. The plots are quite different but both describe time travel. A few years later his short story The Thames Valley Catastrophe (published 1901 in The Strand magazine) describes the destruction of London by a massive volcanic eruption. Whilst the premise now may seem outlandish, at the time genuine panic and concern set in as, like his contemporary, Jules Verne, much of great science fiction writing is rooted in a plausibility that is set out very convincingly.

In detective fiction too his works include female detectives, very much an innovation in the young genre and his gentleman rogue, Colonel Clay, is seen as a forerunner to other, perhaps more famous characters, by other later writers.

In 1881 he had settled at Dorking, where he took great delight in botanical walks in the woods and sandy heaths. He never enjoyed particularly good health and so almost every winter he would depart for milder climes, to winter in the south of Europe, usually at Antibes, though occasionally as far as Algiers and Egypt.

In 1892 he bought land almost on the summit of Hind Head, and built himself a charming cottage which he called the Croft. Here he found that it was possible to endure the vagaries of the English winter and in landscape more beautiful and wilder than at Dorking and that his long scientific training could better appreciate.

His growing re-discovery and interest in art in the later part of his life allowed him to blend together literature, art and history in a series of guide books on Paris, Florence, Venice, and the cities of Belgium.

On October 25th 1899 Grant Allen died at his home in Hindhead, Haslemere, Surrey, England. He died just before finishing Hilda Wade. The novel's final episode, which he dictated to his friend, doctor and neighbour Sir Arthur Conan Doyle from his bed appeared under the appropriate title, The Episode of the Dead Man Who Spoke in the Strand Magazine in 1900.

Grant Allen is rarely heard of today, although an occasional short story can be heard on the radio or reprinted among magazine enthusiasts but in his time he did much to entertain the masses and push several genres along a richer journey they are still proceeding on today.

Physiological Æsthetics. 1877
The Colour-Sense: Its Origin and Development. 1879
Evolutionist at Large. 1881
Vignettes from Nature. 1881
The Colours of Flowers. 1882
Colin Clout's Calendar. 1883
Flowers and Their Pedigrees. 1883
Philistia. 1884
Strange Stories. Short Stories. 1884
Babylon. A novel in 3 volumes. 1885
For Mamie's Sake. 1886
In All Shades. 1886
The Beckoning Hand & Other Stories. 1887
This Mortal Coil: A Novel. 1888
Force and Energy. 1888
The Devil's Die. 1888
The White Man's Foot. 1888
Falling in Love. 1889
The Tents of Shem. 1889
Wednesday the Tenth. 1890
The Great Taboo. 1890
Dumaresq's Daughter. 1891
What's Bred in the Bone. 1891
The Duchess of Powysland. 1892
The Scallywag. 1893
Michael's Crag. 1893
The Lower Slopes. 1894
Post-Prandial Philosophy. 1894
The British Barbarians. 1895
At Market Value. 1895
The Story of the Plants. 1895
The Desire of the Eyes. 1895
The Woman Who Did. 1895
The Jaws of Death. 1896
A Bride from the Desert. 1896
Under Sealed Orders. 1896
Moorland Idylls. 1896
An African Millionaire. Colonel Clay's novel. 1897
The Evolution of the Idea of God. 1897
Paris. 1897
The Type-writer Girl. (as Olive Pratt Rayner) 1897
Tom, Unlimited. (as Martin Leach Warborough) 1897
Flashlights on Nature. 1898
The Incidental Bishop. 1898
Venice. 1898
The European Tour. 1899
A Splendid Sin. 1899
Miss Cayley's Adventures. 1899
Twelve Tales: With a Headpiece, a Tailpiece, and an Intermezzo. 1899

Hilda Wade (finished by Arthur Conan Doyle). 1900
Linnet. 1900
The Backslider. 1901
Sir Theodore's Guest & Other Stories. 1902
Evolution in Italian Art. 1908
The Hand of God. 1909
The Plants. 1909

Short Stories
The Empress of Andorra. 1878
My New Year Among the Mummies. 1878
Lucretia. 1879
My Circular Tour. 1880
A Ballade of Evolution. 1880
Ram Das of Cawnpore. 1880
The Chinese Play at the Haymarket. 1880
The Senior Proctor's Wooing. 1881
Pausodyne. 1881
Caribbean Twelve Per Cents. 1882
An Episode in High Life. 1882
Mr Chung. 1882
Isadine and I. 1883
The Backsider. 1883
The Reverend John Creedy. 1883
The Foundering of the Fortuna. 1883
The Third Time
The Gold Wulfric
My Uncle's Will. 1884
Carvalho. 1884
The Mysterious Occurence in Piccadilly. 1884
Dr Greatex's Engagement. 1884
Hugh Portledown's Return from Normandy. 1884
The Child of Phalanstery. 1884
The Curate of Churnside. 1884
John Cann's Treasure. 1884
Olga Davidoff's Husband. 1884
The Search Party's Find. 1885
The Two Carnegie's. 1885
Professor Milliter's Dilemma. 1885
In Strict Confidence. 1885
The Beckoning Hand. 1885
The Third Time. 1886
Harry's Inheritance. 1886
The Gold Wulfric. 1886
Mr Pierpoint's Repentance. 1886
Claude Tyack's Ordeal. 1887
Leonard's Recovery. 1887
A Social Difficulty. 1887
Dr Palliser's Patient. 1888
My Christmas Eve at Marzin. 1888

The Sultan's Sister. 1888
His First Crime. 1889
The Mayfield Mystery. 1889
Andre Canivet's Curse. 1890
Old Margaret. 1890
My One Gorilla. 1890
Dick Prothero's Luck. 1890
A Deadly Dilemma. 1891
Jerry Stokes. 1891
Selwyn Utterton's Nemesis. 1891
General Passavant's Will. 1891
The Briefless Barrister. 1891
Melissa's Tour. 1891
Karen – A Canadian Romance. 1891
The Prisoner of Assiout. 1891
The Abbe's Repentance. 1891
Masie Bowman's Fate. 1891
Naomi's Christmas Eves. 1891
That Friend of Sylvia's. 1892
The Conscientious Burglar. 1892
The Minor Poet. 1892
The Governor's Story. 1892
The Pot Boiler. 1892
The Great Ruby. 1892
Ewen Murray's Swim. 1892
Ivan Greet's Masterpiece. 1892
Pallinghurst Barrow. 1892
Langalula. 1893
The Assasin's Knife. 1893
The Artist and the Penny-a-Liner. 1893
A Casual Conversation. 1893
How To Succeed in Literature. 1893
Torrigiano. 1893
A Modern Sibyl: A Florentine Sketch. 1893
Nemesis Wins. 1894
Cecca's Lover. 1894
A Self Respecting Servant. 1894
Passiflora Sanguinea. 1894
An Excellent Match. 1894
Major Kinfaun's Marriage. 1894
Grateful Joe. 1894
An Idyll of the Ice. 1894
Criss Cross Love. 1894
Poor Little Soul. 1894
Amour de Voyage. 1894
The Dynamiter's Sweetheart. 1894
A Triumph of Civilisation. 1894
Dr Wardroper's Lie. 1894
The Miraclous Explorer. 1894
Leon and Leonie. 1895
A Comic Emotion. 1895

Joe's Rascality. 1895
Evelyn Moore's Poet. 1895
Frasine's First Communion. 1895
TheDead Man Speaks. 1895
A Study From the Nude. 1895
Cecca's Choice. 1895
The Desire of the Eyes. 1895
The Making of a Poet. 1895
The Man From Cumbrae. 1895
Fogo Skerries. 1895
The Great Californian Heiress. 1895
Cap'n Tom Woolley. 1895
The Girl at the Fair. 1895
Love's Old Dream. 1895
A Modern Pygmalion. 1895
A Bride From the Desert. 1895
The Practical Test. 1896
A Confidential Communication. 1896
The Great Temperance Preacher. 1896
A Day on the River. 1896
The Episode of the Mexican Seer. 1896
A Midsummer Episode. 1896
The Episode of the Diamond Links. 1896
Omar at Marlow. 1896
A Mere Matter of Standpoint. 1896
Fair Exchange. 1896
The Cowardly Dynamiter. 1896
The Episode of the Old Master. 1896
The Episode of the Tyrolean Castle. 1896
Janet's Nemesis. 1896
Entirely Accidental. 1896
The Episode of the Drawn Game. 1896
Wolverden Tower. 1896
The Episode of the German Professor. 1896
The Episode of the Arrest of the Colonel. 1896
The Episode of the Seldom Gold Mine. 1897
The Camisard's Bride. 1897
The Episode of the Japanned Dispatch Box. 1897
Llanfihangel Skerries. 1897
The Episode of the Game of Poker. 1897
The Episode of the Bertillon Method. 1897
A Lady of Florence. 1897
The Episode of the Old Bailey. 1897
A British Verdict. 1897
A Domestic Tragedy. 1897
A College Charm. 1897
A Freak of Memory. 1897
The Judge's Cross. 1897
The Thames Valley Catastrophe. 1897
The Great Oriental Seer. 1897
The Adventures of the Cantankerous Old Lady. 1898

The Adventure of the Supercilious Attache. 1898
The Pirate of Cliveden Reach. 1898
The Adventure of the Amateur Commission. 1898.
The Adventure of the Impromptu Mountaineer. 1898
Joe's Wife. 1898
The Adventure of the Urbane Old Gentleman. 1898
The Adventure of the Unobtrusive Oasis. 1898
The Adventure of the Pea Green Patrician. 1898
Isenberg's Regiment. 1898
The Adventure of the Magnificent Maharajah. 1898
A Woman's Hand: A Story. 1898
The Adventure of the Cross Eyed QC. 1898
The Christmas Eve Concert. 1898
The Adventure of the Oriental Attendant. 1899
Joseph's Dream. 1899
The Adventure of the Unprofessional Detective. 1899
Hobbling Mary. 1899
The Episode of the Patient Who Disappointed Her Doctor. 1899
The Episode of the Gentleman Who Had Failed For Everything. 1899
The Episode of the Wife Who Did Her Duty. 1899
The Episode of the Man Who Would Not Commit Suicide. 1899
A Regrettable Error. 1899
Peace-At-Any-Price Bill. 1899
The Episode of the Letter with a Basingstoke Post-Mark. 1899
The Episode of the Stone That Looked About It. 1899
His Ways Inscrutable. 1899
The Episode of the European With A Kaffir Heart. 1899
The Episode of the Lady Who Was Very Exclusive. 1899
The Episode of the Guide Who Knew the Country. 1899
Luigi and the Salvationist. 1899.
A Christmas Adventure. 1899.
The Episode of the Officer Who Understood Perfectly. 1900
Meriel Stanley, Poacher. 1900
The Episode of the Dead Man Who Spoke. 1900
A Question of Colour. 1900
Fra Benedett's Medal: A Story. 1900
The Temple of Fate: A Fable. 1900
The Way to Keronan. 1902
Lucy Lockett. 1902
Spencerian. 1904

Articles

1878. Hellas and Civilization, Gentleman's Magazine, Vol. CCXLIII
1878. Nation-making: A Theory of National Characters, Gentleman's Magazine, Vol. CCXLIII
1878. The Origin of Fruits, in Popular Science Monthly Volume 13
1879. Why Do We Eat our Dinner? in Popular Science Monthly Volume 14
1879. A Problem in Human Evolution, in Popular Science Monthly Volume
1879. Pleased with a Feather, in Popular Science Monthly Volume 15
1880. Why Keep India? The Contemporary Review, Vol. XXXVIII
1880. The Growth of Sculpture, The Cornhill Magazine, Vol. XLII

1880. The English Chronicle, Gentleman's Magazine, Vol. CCXLV
1880. The Venerable Bede, Gentleman's Magazine, Vol. CCXLIX
1880. The Dog's Universe, Gentleman's Magazine, Vol. CCXLIX
1880. Evolution and Geological Time, Gentleman's Magazine, Vol. CCXLIX
1880. Geology and History, in Popular Science Monthly Volume 17
1880. Aesthetic Feeling in Birds, in Popular Science Monthly Volume 17
1880. Aesthetic Evolution in Man, in Popular Science Monthly Volume 18
1881. The Story of Wulfgeat, Gentleman's Magazine, Vol. CCLI
1882. An English Shire, Gentleman's Magazine, Vol. CCLII
1882. The Welsh in the West Country, Gentleman's Magazine, Vol. CCLIII
1882. The Colours of Flowers, The Cornhill Magazine, Vol. XLV
1882. An English Weed, The Cornhill Magazine, Vol. XLV
1882. Sir Charles Lyell, in Popular Science Monthly Volume 20
1882. Hyacinth-Bulbs, in Popular Science Monthly Volume 20
1882. Who was Primitive Man? in Popular Science Monthly Volume 22
1883. The Pedigree of Wheat, in Popular Science Monthly Volume 22
1883. From Buttercups to Monk's-Hood, in Popular Science Monthly Volume 23
1883. Honeysuckle, Gentleman's Magazine, Vol. CCLV
1884. The Garden Snail, Gentleman's Magazine, Vol. CCLVI
1884. Our Debt to Insects, Gentleman's Magazine, Vol. CCLVI
1884. Idiosyncrasy, in Popular Science Monthly Volume 24
1884. The Ancestry of Birds, in Popular Science Monthly Volume 24
1884. The Milk in the Cocoa-Nut, in Popular Science Monthly Volume 25
1884. Our Debt to Insects, in Popular Science Monthly Volume 25
1884. Hickory-Nuts and Butternuts, in Popular Science Monthly Volume 25
1884. Queer Flowers, in Popular Science Monthly Volume 26
1885. Food and Feeding, in Popular Science Monthly Volume 26
1885. Concerning Clover, in Popular Science Monthly Volume 28
1886. A Thinking Machine, Gentleman's Magazine, Vol. CCLX
1886. Fish Out of Water, in Popular Science Monthly Volume 28
1886. A Thinking Machine, in Popular Science Monthly Volume 28
1886. Thistles, in Popular Science Monthly Volume 30, November 1886
1887. A Mount Washington Sandwort, in Popular Science Monthly Volume 30
1887. Among the Thousand Islands, in Popular Science Monthly Volume 31
1887. The Progress of Science from 1836 to 1886, in Popular Science Monthly Volume 31
1887. American Cinque-Foils, in Popular Science Monthly Volume 32
1888. Gourds and Bottles, in Popular Science Monthly Volume 33
1888. A Living Mystery, in Popular Science Monthly Volume 33
1888. Evolving the Camel, in Popular Science Monthly Volume 34
1889. From Africa, Gentleman's Magazine, Vol. CCLXVII
1889. Genius and Talent, in Popular Science Monthly Volume 34
1889. Plain Words on the Woman Question, in Popular Science Monthly Volume 36
1890. The Girl of the Future, Universal Review, Vol. VII.
1891. Democracy and Diamonds, The Contemporary Review, Vol. LIX
1892. A Desert Fruit, in Popular Science Monthly Volume 41
1893. Ghost Worship and Tree Worship I, in Popular Science Monthly Volume 42
1893. Ghost Worship and Tree Worship II, in Popular Science Monthly Volume 42
1897. Spencer and Darwin, in Popular Science Monthly Volume 50
1898. The Romance of Race, in Popular Science Monthly Volume 53
1898. The Season of the Year, in Popular Science Monthly Volume 54

Grant Allen wrote various poems published in many magazines etc. We have not listed them here but hope to record some of them in the future.

www.ingramcontent.com/pod-product-compliance
Lightning Source LLC
Chambersburg PA
CBHW061505170626
46811CB00004B/1612